THE
HORSEMAN
OF
SLEEPY HOLLOW

by REBECCA F. KENNEY

This book is a work of fiction. Names, characters, places, and incidents are the product of the author's imagination or are used fictitiously. Any resemblance to actual events, locales, or persons, living or dead, is coincidental.

Copyright © 2021 by Rebecca F. Kenney

All rights reserved. In accordance with the U.S. Copyright Act of 1976, the scanning, uploading, and electronic sharing of any part of this book without the permission of the publisher is unlawful piracy and theft of the author's intellectual property. If you would like to use material from the book (other than for review purposes), prior written permission must be obtained by contacting the publisher at rfkenney@gmail.com. Thank you for your support of the author's rights.

First Edition: October 2021

Kenney, Rebecca F.
The Horseman of Sleepy Hollow / by Rebecca F. Kenney—First edition.

PLAYLIST

"Man in the Mirror" J2 Version feat. Cameron the Public (orig. Michael Jackson)

"Animal" J2 Epic Trailer Version feat. Keeley Bumford

"Closer" Epic Trailer Version feat. Keeley Bumford

"Halo" J2 Epic Trailer Version feat. I.Am.Willow

"Umbrella" J2 Epic Trailer Version feat. JVZEL

"Don't Fear the Reaper" The Spiritual Machines

"Passion Colors Everything" Poets of the Fall

"Bad Romance" J2 Epic Stripped Version

"Deep Sweet Dreams" Umea Bodo

"Change on the Rise" Avi Kaplan

"I'm Not Afraid" Tommee Profitt

"You Belong to Me" Cat Pierce

"Physical" Dua Lipa

AUTHOR'S NOTE

This novel is inspired by and based upon Washington Irving's "The Legend of Sleepy Hollow," first published in 1820. However, the story has been entirely rebuilt and re-imagined. I have made an effort to be historically accurate wherever possible, but the storytelling and the romance take precedence over the accuracy of historical detail and dialogue. The book is also not intended to perfectly replicate the topography of the actual village of Sleepy Hollow in Mount Pleasant, New York.

1

Such an odd thing, the human head.

The center of all thought and impulse, of emotion and intelligence, set atop a column so slender that an awkward fall could snap it. Its construction, the way it joined to the body, was either an incredibly elegant design, or a rather foolish one. I could not decide which.

In this rosy gown, with my golden curls pulled halfway up, my neck looked altogether too slim to support my own head. But perhaps its fragility fit my appearance—the perfect Dutch doll, all curves and dimples, ready to be trotted out before my suitors again. I smiled at my reflection, gritting my teeth so hard my jaw ached.

What did my skull look like under my creamy skin and pink cheeks? I tried to imagine it—my pert nose disappearing, the flesh melting away. I would be an egg-shaped shell of bone, with a couple of empty eyeholes, delicate ridges of cheekbone, and grinning jaws.

"That dress is too low-cut, Katrina." My mother's voice startled me out of my dark thoughts. "I have always said so. It is not right for a God-fearing girl to wear such a thing."

I smiled, tracing my fingers over the tops of my breasts. They swelled upward with every inhale, a vision that would draw certain male eyes to me on this night. "I am no girl, Mother. At twenty, I am a woman."

She clucked her tongue at me, tugging the neckline up, moving the lace higher onto my shoulders. "You should be married by now, Katrina. You need to make up your mind, before your charms fade."

"I thought you wanted me to cover up my charms. Really, Mother, you should make up your mind."

My mother cupped my face in her hands, a little too tightly for comfort. "Katrina. You must accept a proposal soon. Once you are settled, no one will have reason to gossip about you."

I stepped back, pushing her hands away from my cheeks. "People talk about me?"

"They wonder why you are not yet married, why you continue to turn down proposals or ask young men to wait while you decide. I hear the whispers constantly, how you are a fearful coquette, a tease, a siren—" She

drew out a delicate handkerchief and pressed it to her mouth, her eyes turning pink and watery. "Such rumors, Katrina. I will not have my only child spoken of in such a manner."

"And if I choose one of these fine country lads, the rumors will cease?" I arched an eyebrow.

"You will need to dress more modestly once you are married." My mother frowned at the scandalous length of my petticoat, which revealed my entire foot and ankle. "And you may not gallivant about the countryside with your friends, or tromp 'round with the farm hands, or run about on your own. You will need to stay quietly at home and tend to the affairs of the house, and set your attention to spinning and needlework."

"I do not 'gallivant,'" I protested. "And if I follow the farm hands around, it is because I want to learn all I can about how to run this place properly."

"Your husband will tend to that, once you are married."

"And whom would you have me choose?" I looked her straight in the eye, though I knew the answer she would give.

"Brom Van Brunt is a strapping and worthy man," she said. "Strong and keen-minded in matters of the land."

"You have been pushing him at me since I could speak." I wrinkled my nose, poking at the few freckles sprinkled across it.

My mother caught the expression. "You do not wear your bonnet as often as you should. And you do not listen to me now any better than you did when you were five, or ten, or eighteen. Yes, I would have you marry Brom. He is the best match in Sleepy Hollow—in the whole valley, or the towns beyond."

"And you are great friends with his mother."

Anika Van Brunt and my mother had been inseparable all their lives. They loved to tell us, their only children, how they were pregnant at the same time and gave birth on the same day, one at dawn and the other at dusk. Superstition flourished in Sleepy Hollow, trickling along its streambeds, hovering in quiet glades, whispering through the evening smoke from our chimneys, trailing misty fingers across the ponds and rain barrels each morning. And so it seemed to my parents, and to Brom's, that their children were destined to be paired forever.

If I had merely wanted a handsome man, with arms like a Greek god and the height of a hero, Brom would have been the man. He was striking in aspect, with prominent cheekbones jutting above the swath of his blond beard, and hair the color of ripe wheat waving down to his shoulders. He reminded me of a Viking of old—or what I imagined a Viking might look like. And his eyes—such an astonishing blue, vivid as the autumn sky over the orchard on a clear day. He and I made a gorgeous pair. With his physical strength and determined spirit, he could one day help me maintain and grow all the wealth my father had amassed.

Brom was the ideal choice for my husband. Which was why I resisted committing to the match, despite my amicable relationship with him.

"My friendship with his mother aside, he is perfect for you, Katrina," said my mother. She tucked away her handkerchief. "Come, enough preening. We must receive our guests."

"For the quilting frolic. Tell me, will there be any actual quilting, or merely a vast amount of matchmaking?"

My mother swatted my arm as we passed out of the bedroom together. "Mind yourself, Katrina Van Tassel.

Remember who you are, and try not to shame us. Give Brom the assurance he deserves—the promise of his place in your heart. I have it on good authority that he may ask for your hand sometime tonight. If he proposes, you must accept."

She swept on ahead of me, leaving me no chance to argue.

"On good authority," I muttered. "From his mother, no doubt."

Not that I bore her any real ill will. Anika Van Brunt was a soft, sweet dumpling of a woman with a cloud of pale curls, like a halo around her smiling face. I liked her because she was not afraid to laugh, loud and long, even at jokes that made my mother blush. I wondered if her status as a widow gave her a little more freedom to enjoy such things. If her husband were alive, would he have laid a hand on her arm and instructed her to be silent? No one would ever tell me much about Cor Van Brunt, Brom's father. The gossips and schoolboys of Sleepy Hollow circulated a dozen stories about how he had met his end, each more fanciful than the last, until I no longer knew what was truth.

One element most of the stories shared was Cor Van Brunt's lack of a head when he was found. Some said wolves attacked him. Others blamed the woman in white, a spirit who was rumored to haunt the deepest places of the wood. But the most salacious of the tales blamed the elder Van Brunt's death on a shade with a particular connection to Sleepy Hollow—the Headless Horseman. Tales of the Horseman's gory deeds predated the colonies' war for independence. Some said he was a bold and bloody Hessian who slaughtered scores of men until a cannon blasted off his head.

The idea that the ghost of a battle-dead Hessian stole the head of Brom's father never rang true with me. Yet I had never dared to ask Brom or his mother for the real story. I did not wish to press an old wound and cause them pain.

As I moved into the front hall of our sprawling home, I saw Anika Van Brunt greeting my mother. Her smile broadened when she noticed me, and I found myself smiling in return. She held a basket full of quilting squares and supplies, and behind her towered Brom with two more covered baskets, probably packed with delectable treats for the evening's festivities.

The sight of Brom triggered a frightened flutter in my stomach. If he asked for my hand this evening, I could not refuse him outright without shaming him and his mother, and enraging my own parents.

If he did have plans to propose tonight, I must do my best to avoid him.

He made as if to approach me, but then his mother and mine steered him off to the kitchen to deposit his baskets.

And while he was gone, my salvation arrived, in the spindly shape of the schoolmaster, Ichabod Crane.

Ah, Ichabod. He stalked the lanes and meadows like a strutting rooster, proud of his flock of mediocre students, whom he flogged with disturbing regularity. He had a large nose and a low forehead, a thinning mop of lank brown hair, and a body that stayed rail-thin no matter how much he ate—and the man could eat. My mother always sighed and checked the larder's stock every time she saw Ichabod approaching our home, which he had done often of late, under the guise of teaching me how to sing.

Today he looked especially awkward, with a lumpy cravat knotted at his neck, draped in a fine greatcoat he must have borrowed for the occasion.

"Miss Katrina!" He sauntered over to me, his pale green eyes sparkling with excitement. "Such a merry gathering this will be! I hope I may claim the honor of your company for a dance or two!"

"You may have all of them, Ichabod," I said recklessly. "And call me Katrina."

Ichabod swallowed hard, his Adam's apple bobbing dramatically. "It isn't proper, miss."

"But I command it, and therefore you must obey."

"Of—of course, Miss—I mean, Katrina."

"Good boy." I leaned in and kissed his cheek—just a peck, but he reacted as if I had slapped him, pressing his palm to his face and looking completely overcome.

His reaction delighted me.

To be truthful, I liked playing with my suitors when they came to visit. If the gossips of Sleepy Hollow knew half of the wicked things I did, my reputation would be ruined.

When Brom passed time with me, I loved watching his cheeks redden and his eyes burn as my fingers crept over his thigh underneath the book we pretended to read. My father, who would often smoke his pipe at the other end of the piazza, had never noticed. And I took care to only touch Brom's thigh, never letting my fingertips creep further inward.

I loved the way Ichabod's voice would lurch into a higher register when I ran a finger along the neckline of my dress and tugged it ever so slightly lower while he was giving me my singing lesson under the elm tree.

I played similar games with the other men who came courting—whispers and stray touches—seemingly accidental, always intentional. It was a kind of power, one that I craved. But it was never quite enough, because I did not love any of them.

Maybe, if I could have mashed Brom and the schoolmaster together into one man—Brom's height, strength, and good looks, along with Ichabod's intelligence, voice, and dancing skills—then I would have had the perfect man, one worthy of my body and heart. But I knew no such convenient magic.

Brom emerged from the kitchen, so I seized Ichabod's elbow and ushered him out the front door. "You must come and see the ducks and the geese, Ichabod. They are fatter than ever, and will make for delicious holiday feasting this year. And the squashes and pumpkins have grown since you last visited—they are immense, truly! Come and look at them."

"Of course, dear Katrina, of course!" He hurried along beside me, waving amiably to the other neighbors who were arriving.

I had known he would not protest a tour of the farm. After all, Ichabod was more in love with our land, our wealth, and our house than he was with me. Avarice had glowed in his eyes from the moment he set foot in our home, shortly after his arrival in Sleepy Hollow. On that first day, he ogled the neatly-hung tools along the piazza and eyed the china and silver in the parlor's corner cupboards. He had looked at my figure and at my family's glossy furniture with the same degree of lust.

And yet I could not hate him. He was so very earnest about everything, so intent on working hard and making everyone in the valley like him. He was a man who came from little, with an eye to making much of himself by sheer force of will. I could not help but respect his ambition.

Ichabod tugged on the lapels of his coat, squaring his shoulders as if walking at my side were the greatest honor in the world. Or perhaps he was imagining himself as the proud owner of all that he saw. Clearly he had taken pains to look his best this evening.

"Your boots are so brightly polished," I remarked. "How did you keep them so clean during the long walk here?"

"I did not come on foot," he said, lifting his chin. "I came on Hans Van Ripper's horse, Gunpowder."

"What?" I smothered a laugh with my hand. "Gunpowder? That old firebrand is more devil than horse. He is more likely to throw you than to see you safely home, Ichabod. You must borrow one of our horses for the return trip."

"No, no." Ichabod shook his head. "I promised to return Gunpowder to his stable, safe and sound, and that is what I will do. What is a man, if his word cannot be trusted?" He opened his pale eyes very wide, as if to indicate that I should take special note of what he just said.

"I agree. An honest and trustworthy man is a treasure, to be sure." I laid my hands on the top rail of the wooden fence and admired the plump-breasted ducks waddling beside the pond. The blue of the autumn sky colored the water azure and flecked it with snowy mirror images of the clouds overhead. Every bush rustled with twittering sparrows and robins, and from the tree across the pond echoed the shrill cry of a blue jay claiming his territory. Though the sun was warm, the breeze caressing my face carried the sharpness of coming frost.

And then something else caressed my arm—the long narrow fingers of Ichabod Crane.

"Katrina, I have something I would ask you," he muttered.

My heart dropped with dread. In avoiding one proposal, I had walked into another.

Ichabod opened his thin lips to say more, but at that moment music unfurled from the house, rippling across the fences and fields. Violins, fifes, and fiddles mingled in a melody too tempting to ignore.

"Ichabod!" I exclaimed, so loudly that he startled. "Shall we go and dance?"

"But—"

"You may ask me your question later," I said quietly, smiling at him and blinking my lashes. "But first, let us enjoy merriment and food with our family and friends."

"Our—family—" Ichabod's eyes glazed over with rapture. He did not speak as I hustled him back toward the house.

Of course I was deceiving him, leading him on. But he and Brom—they were forcing me into it, with their incessant pursuit of my affection. Some of the books I devoured secretly by night portrayed it as a very fine thing for a woman to have two suitors. The more men circling the heroine, the better, or so the stories hinted. But the reality of it was not very romantic. A constant fog of tension dulled the conversation whenever Brom and Ichabod were under the same roof. Even when I was with one of them, the shadow of the other loomed over our interactions. Each man spoke to me carefully, consciously, trying to impress me, trying to ferret out what traits of his rival I found most attractive so he could endeavor to emulate or surpass them.

It was exhausting.

When Ichabod and I entered the house, we found the second-best parlor already cleared for dancing. My father caught my eye and beckoned me forward. The flush of his cheeks told me he had already dipped into the good ale.

"Everyone! Here is my fair daughter, Katrina! Is she not beautiful? A worthy heir to all I own, alongside a good sturdy husband of course!" He knocked elbows with Brom, who stood nearby, frowning at the sight of me on Ichabod's arm.

"A good sturdy husband is a wondrous thing," I said. "But I am not married yet! And now, we dance!"

The other young lads and lasses of the valley cheered my answer. I whirled Ichabod into the center of the room and we began to dance, while other couples gravitated toward us like chickens to feed.

If I could have stolen the fire in Ichabod's feet for myself, I would have done it. The man transformed under the power of music. His lanky body turned loose and disjointed in the best way, curving sinuous as a snake, then snapping upright—his feet tapped a rapid beat against the floor—all his stiff manners were forgotten, lost in the joy of the dance. In his company I could let myself go too, swaying my hips and twisting my body in ways that the gossips would no doubt discuss over their tea and mending for weeks to follow. Ichabod and I were lightning, bursting white and hot in this sleepy circle of simple folk with their modest twirls and careful steps.

Whenever I danced with him, I wondered if maybe he was the right choice after all. If only I could ignore his harshness with his students, his lust for my father's property, and the foolish remarks he often made in company. If only he could always be like this, a demon of the dance, wild and untethered.

But when the music ended, he reverted to the prim schoolmaster, blinking and nodding to those who applauded his performance, visibly swelling with pride. When he looked at me, his eyes glistened with the certainty that he was rising in the world, that he was mere inches from claiming the prize he sought.

Me. I was the prize. The necessary accessory to wealth, and position, and generations of his progeny to grace the glades of Sleepy Hollow. I imagined our children—snipe-necked little things with pale eyes and lank hair like Ichabod. In my mind's eye they all looked like Ichabod, and none of them were like me.

After the dancing, we wandered to the long tables set up throughout the house and on the piazza. The good people of Sleepy Hollow knew how to throw a party. Roast chickens sat on trays, surrounded by steaming potatoes and carrots. There were platters of smoked beef and sliced ham, trays of frosted ginger cakes and golden fried doughnuts, bowls of pears and peaches and plums swimming in sugary juice, plates of grilled fish dripping in butter and sprinkled with sprigs of herbs, and pies issuing fruit-scented steam through their latticework of crust.

 Ichabod practically drooled over the spread. He began heaping a plate, piling scoopfuls of potatoes atop slices of meat atop wedges of pie. Clearly he would not be filling a plate for his dance partner, so I took a plate myself and selected a few strips of beef, some peas and carrots, and a crisply cut slice of pumpkin pie, dripping with fresh cream. Then I walked through the house, searching for a quiet corner where I could enjoy my meal in peace.

 Unfortunately all the rooms were filled with wrinkled, sharp-eyed grandmothers and lace-bedecked goodwives and jolly farmers. Children frolicked through the halls, rushing past the tables to snag sweets and then racing out the back door, hollering with victory. I followed the children outside to the back of the house and perched on the end of an upturned log, barely caring that my party dress would probably be smudged.

 The children were playing some complicated version of tag amid circles of rope on the ground—a game I had not seen before. As I watched, I noticed one boy hunched into his coat collar, crooking his fingers into claws and chasing the others until they ran squealing into a rope circle for safety. One of the girls had draped a white scarf over her hair and trailed after the others, wailing. When she touched one of them, they had to freeze in place until the count of ten.

"The Horseman is coming, the Horseman is coming!" chanted the children in the circle. They broke and ran, while the boy in the coat loped after them.

The rules made no sense to me, but the vigor and joy in their faces made me smile.

Behind the children, above the golden fields and the jagged black line of the forest, violent streaks of color slashed the sky—a bloodbath of orange and dark purple and crimson. A brisk wind scoured across the worn dirt of the back yard, sending a fine layer of dust over my dancing shoes. I shivered and rose from the stump to carry my empty plate back inside.

"Are you hiding, Katrina?" Brom appeared in the doorway, blocking my path.

"I was watching the children play. It is endearing." I forced a smile and made as if to move past him.

He side-stepped, his broad chest inches from mine. "You should dance with me now."

"The dancing is over, Brom. And I'm tired."

"No doubt, with that display of yours. I hope you do not plan to make a fool of yourself in that way once you are a married woman."

"What can I say? I love to dance."

"A married woman may dance, with restraint. Not with such abandon, such suggestive movements." He flicked the lace at the neckline of my dress. "Men will get the wrong idea."

I was about to respond, but a couple of Brom's usual companions shouted to him from across the yard, lifting a bottle they had doubtless purloined from my father's store. Brom grinned his approval and raised his hand in response.

"I would speak with you later, Katrina," he said. Then he went to join his friends, and I escaped inside.

Ichabod was clearing what was probably his second or third plate. I snatched it from him and grabbed his elbow as a knight might grab his trusty shield. "Come with me. The dancing is over—let us find something else amusing to do."

"But—there is still plenty of food—" Ichabod eyed the tables as I dragged him toward the front door.

"I will send you some of the leftovers tomorrow. Come."

"Very well." He cleared his throat noisily. "I had something to ask you anyway—a quiet moment alone will not be unwelcome."

Oh, good heavens. Was my entire evening to be ruined by lovesick idiots? I needed another distraction, and quickly.

I burst out of the front door and hurried down the steps of the piazza with Ichabod in tow, waving briefly to my father and several gentlemen who were smoking their pipes in the blue-gray gloom. Their faces glowed ruddy and joyful in the golden light from the house windows.

Out on the front lawn, the long shadows of the house, the out-buildings, and the trees had already darkened the landscape. Some of the boys, ranging in age from sixteen to nineteen or so, had started a fire in the stone pit near one of the barns. I tugged Ichabod toward it, eager to be among other people where he could not easily propose marriage to me.

Among those around the fire were a few of my dearest friends—we had played together as children and were as familiar as family now. Vajèn, a girl of eighteen with rosy cheeks and brown ringlets as glossy as a ripe acorn's shell. Maria, seventeen, skinny and pale, her knees bouncing with excess energy. Sascha, sixteen years old, with her flat blond hair in thin plaits and her wide green eyes fixed on Ichabod.

Out here, far from the older adults' judgmental eyes, some of my father's younger servants could join us without fear of rebuke. I was glad to see everyone sitting companionably together around the fire pit.

"Katrina, you are just in time!" Vajèn hailed me, her eyes sparkling. "The boys are telling tales of hauntings and murder and witches—such dreadfully lurid stories. You must hear them."

"Delightful," I replied. "But I will warn you, it is difficult to frighten me. I do not give credence to such tales."

Ichabod clutched my arm. "You do not believe in the presence of spirits, or the power of the occult?"

"Perhaps a little, I suppose—but ghostly riders? Witches who can turn people into toads? Spirits who do nothing but hang about in glades, waiting for travelers to pass by? It sounds dreadfully boring. If I were a spirit, I would float through the whole world and see the sights, instead of moping about in one place."

"But spirits are tethered to the spot where they died." Ichabod's voice turned shrill with eagerness.

"And witches are capable of much more than toads. Half a moment, I want to show you something." He raced away, into the dark, toward the stables.

"What can he be going to fetch?" giggled Vajèn.

"I have no idea." I stared into the fire, hoping they would not expect me to make any further excuses for him. Life as Ichabod's wife would doubtless be one long chain of apologies for his odd behavior. Not that I minded his vagaries myself—but we would have to live among the people of Sleepy Hollow, and they preferred people who moved slowly and performed in ways that were both expected and respectable.

"How long will you keep Brom and the schoolmaster at odds, Katrina?" Sascha's green eyes fixed on mine. "Their rivalry is growing beyond all decency."

"It is." Our young servant Lucas's deep voice issued from the dark. He moved into the circle of amber firelight and swung one leg over the bench on which Vajèn sat. When she did not protest, he seated himself. "I heard that Van Brunt has been harassing the schoolmaster, stopping up the chimney of the schoolhouse, breaking into the place at night and stacking up the furniture this way and that, giving the students popguns to interrupt the lessons."

"Harmless pranks," I replied. "Annoying, to be sure, but Brom's jokes do no real damage."

"Maybe not to some of you," Lucas said. "Others are not so blessed. There's a man I know would have lost his leg to a prank of Mister Van Brunt's, had it not been for the Night Angel."

"The Night Angel?" I tilted my head, confused.

"A man who visits the servants sometimes, in the night, especially those who cannot afford a physician. He gives medicine for fevers, pulls the rotting teeth, applies salve to festering wounds." Lucas tossed a twig into the fire. "None of us know his real name, so we call him the Night Angel. He's doing the Lord's work, for sure."

"I don't know about pranks, or about any *angel*," Sascha intercepted. "But, Katrina, if you intend to choose Brom, you should let Ichabod go, so he can choose someone else." Then she clamped her lips shut after the remark, as if she had said more than she meant to.

Desperation clutched my heart. I had thought I would have more time to choose, that I could hold the two of them off a while longer. What was I waiting for? A third option? The longer I waited, the more my reputation as a coquette was solidified in the minds of my friends. The firelight hardened their faces into masks of orange and gray, and when I looked into those faces, I saw condemnation, not sympathy.

It was time to face the facts. No third choice was likely to present itself. No handsome stranger would appear to save me from selecting either Ichabod or Brom.

I was about to respond, but my words were cut off by a whoop and several shouts from somewhere in the night. Brom and a few of his usual companions tramped out of the shadows, hauling Ichabod along by the collar of his coat.

"Lost your walking stick, have you, Katrina?" Brom's eyes were two blue flames, hot and vindictive. "See, I have brought him to you."

I leaped up and ran over to Brom, stroking his sleeve and laughing prettily. "Such a wit you are, Brom. Let him alone now. We were telling ghost stories, and he has brought something to show us."

Brom looked down at me, and I smiled winsomely into his face, while my heart growled unrepentant. He released Ichabod, and the schoolmaster hunched his coat back into place.

"I happened to have a rather interesting book in my saddlebag—Cotton Mather's *History of New England Witchcraft*," Ichabod said. "It holds some fascinating information about the occult, and spirits, and magic of every kind! The owner before me made some additional notes and pasted in a few extra pages, on which you can see records of various wondrous creatures that roam the dark places of the world—" He flung open the book and pointed to an image of a black goat. "Like this, the pooka or shapeshifter of Irish tales. There is even a mention of a headless rider—see? The dullahan, bringer of death. It is said that a dullahan will—"

Brom groaned aloud. "Dullahan? *Dull*, for certain—I have never heard such dry delivery of any story. Enough with your dull old tales, before I fold you up and lay you upon a shelf in your own schoolhouse!" He clapped Ichabod's book shut and tossed it away into the gloom. Then he advanced into the firelight, wedging his broad frame onto the bench between Lucas and Vajèn. "I will tell you a better tale, one that will set your teeth on edge. Come, schoolmaster, sit down and listen. Perhaps

Katrina will let you sit on her lap if the bench is too hard for that bony rump of yours."

I shot Brom a reproachful glare and plunked down onto a bench. Ichabod gingerly seated himself beside me, his thin hands writhing with nerves. He probably wanted to go and look for his precious book, but he dared not disobey Brom's directive. Brom could be a delight, full of jokes and good cheer; but in such a mood as this, it was best not to cross him.

"Ah, the Headless Horseman." Brom's grin dripped with malevolence. "Most often spotted on the Old Church Bridge, where it arches over the deepest and darkest part of the stream. You walk over that bridge on your way back to Van Ripper's place, do you not, Ichabod?"

Ichabod's throat bobbed. "I ride back that way, yes."

"Ride? You have a horse then?"

"Borrowed from Hans Van Ripper. He is called Gunpowder."

"Indeed? I have heard that old plowhorse was a right devil in his day. We must have a race, you and I— you on Gunpowder, and me on Daredevil."

Daredevil was Brom's restive stallion. Brom loved wild things, and he had no greater pleasure than the taming of a savage dog, a fierce hawk, or an unbroken horse. I had often wondered if he thought of me in the same way—as an overly exuberant creature in need of his strong hand. A wild thing to be cowed into submission.

"Daredevil is a much younger horse than Gunpowder," I interjected. "It would not be a fair race."

"Kind, fair-minded Katrina," sneered Brom. "Of course, you are right. It would not be fair to expect Ichabod's old knock-kneed mount to beat the steed who outran the Headless Horseman."

A series of gasps raced around the fire pit. Brom nodded, pleased with the response. "Oh yes. I have encountered the Horseman myself. As you know, sightings of the Horseman used to be commonplace in our grandparents' time. Then he disappeared for a while, until he was seen again, just five years ago, around the time of my father's death."

I caught my breath and gripped the edge of the bench. Was Brom about to tell us the truth about his father's passing?

He continued in a low, sonorous tone."Since then, various sightings have occurred, sometimes resulting in deaths, and sometimes not. You remember the man from the city a few years ago, who passed through with his solicitor and attempted to buy up some of our land?"

Heads nodded all around the circle.

"Well, that gentleman and the solicitor turned up dead a year later—that is to say, their skeletons were found in the wood, picked clean of flesh, with their vital organs gnawed out—and both were lacking skulls."

Beside me, Ichabod let out a terrified wheeze.

Brom's teeth gleamed orange in the glow of the flames. "And then there was the case of old Brouwer. As you know, he has always denied the existence of spirits and ghosts—until one night, not twelve months ago, when he was returning from a market day. He was riding upon his empty cart, counting his coin from the day's commerce, when a flaming pumpkin soared past his shoulder and wheeled away into the trees. Old Brouwer's nag took fright and bucked, knocking Brouwer off the cart and into the road, while his coins rained down around him. The nag charged away, out of sight and beyond recall. Old Brouwer had twisted his leg, but he crawled around as best he could, feeling for the coins in the dark, scraping them together. And whom do you think should come galloping down the road at that very moment?"

Ichabod's skinny fingers gripped my arm, just above the elbow.

"The Horseman," breathed Vajèn.

"Yes, my dear Vajèn—the Headless Horseman. Big as a giant, on a steed hulking and monstrous, with no face above his shoulders, for he carried his head in his hand!"

Sascha squealed and grabbed Ichabod's arm so that the three of us were linked.

"Old Brouwer tried to limp away, sobbing and stuffing his coins into his pockets. But the Horseman rode up to him and reached down, grabbing Brouwer by the neck, and hauled him up onto the saddle behind him. Brouwer nearly fainted from the terror of riding behind the headless ghost. When they came to the bridge, Brouwer saw one chance to save himself. He leaped from the horse's back, over the side of the bridge, and into the brook. He swears that the Horseman's body shook all over, and that he threw off his coat to reveal a skeleton beneath it! Then he disappeared in a flash of fire and a peal of thunder. Brouwer barely had sense enough to swim to shore and limp the rest of the way home."

"But dullahan are not skeletons," squeaked Ichabod. "They look like any man or woman, until they are summoned for a direful deed, and then they—"

"Have you encountered the Headless Horseman?" Brom interrupted, leaning forward. "Have you challenged him to a race, and lived to tell the tale?"

"No," faltered Ichabod.

"Tell us the tale," begged Vajèn.

"It happened just last week." Brom's voice returned to its mysterious cadence. "I was riding back from visiting Katrina. The wind rushed cold through the trees, and I shivered—but I thought I saw sparks on the air, as if carried from a campfire—and a puff of heat passed over my head. Then I saw him, approaching me on his giant horse—the Headless Rider. I knew I had one chance to save myself, or he would take my head." Brom pressed a hand to his jaw, and the girls all sighed in unison. I rolled my eyes.

"Losing my head would be a great sadness, not only for me, but for everyone in Sleepy Hollow," Brom continued. "So I shouted to the Horseman, 'I will race you for a bowl of punch!' He did not answer, but raised one gloved hand, and I knew my challenge had been accepted. We ranged up our horses, side by side, and I saw the horrible red flesh of the Horseman's severed neck, with the white bone of the spine protruding from it. At his belt was a whip made from human spines, and in his hand he wielded a great golden scythe."

"No more," whispered Ichabod. "Please, no more."

Brom ignored him. "We spurred our horses and raced ahead, through the dark forest. Daredevil gave me his best speed ever, for I believe he understood our peril. The Horseman's mount began to lag, and I knew I would win. The Horseman would be obliged to buy me a bowl of punch, and I would have finally overcome the most fearsome legend of our valley. But as we approached the Old Church Bridge, the Horseman's steed reared up and leaped straight over the side, disappearing into the shadows below. I can only assume he was too proud to acknowledge himself beaten."

Ichabod lurched to his feet, disengaging himself from Sascha's grasp. "I—I must look for my book," he stammered, and wobbled away from the fire circle.

Brom stretched out his long legs and smiled. "Some men are too fragile for such tales. Too fragile for anything, I'll wager, including the spawning of heirs." He looked straight at me.

It was a coarse thing to say, probably fueled by ale and jealousy. He would certainly not have said it within earshot of our parents.

My face flaming, I gathered my skirts and marched away from the circle to look for Ichabod.

I found him some distance away, collecting his volume of Cotton Mather's writings from the damp grass.

"Is your book all right?" I asked.

"It is, thank you, Katrina."

I reached out to brush dirt from the spine of the tome, and in doing so, I accidentally brushed over his fingers in the dark. Immediately he shifted the book under his arm and took my hand in his.

"I am sorry for the way Brom treats you," I murmured, trying to gently slide my fingers away—but Ichabod only clutched them tighter.

"Your kindness makes up for his persecutions," Ichabod said. "You are the kindest soul in Sleepy Hollow, Katrina. I have no doubt that your attentions to me on this night were meant to reveal your true feelings—your affection for me. And I would be remiss if I did not return those affections. I am convinced we would be happy together—who could not be, with such wealth and beauty all around us? The riches of this place are beyond compare, and you are the greatest treasure of them all. But I am not without treasures, too—treasures of the mind, of learning, of knowledge—of music, song, and dance—all of which will make me a most interesting daily companion and will help me to efficiently manage this great estate when your father's health eventually fails. And so I come to the reason for my frequent visits here—Katrina Van Tassel, I offer you my hand in marriage. Together we could live in peace and comfort all our lives. This beautiful house and its lands will never need to change. We can keep it perfect, just as it is, and leave it to our children one day."

    While he spoke, my teeth found my lip and ground into it; the pain centered me, clarified my thoughts. "Ichabod, I truly have affection for you, as a good friend. But I am not sure that we could be as happy as you say. There are things I want to do—changes I would make to this place—"

    I could not continue. Ichabod had no home of his own, but stayed with various families by turns, and so he was naturally a purveyor of gossip. I could not trust him to keep my convictions private until I was ready to share them.

"I need time to think," I said. "My mind is not yet made up."

Ichabod jerked his hand away. "But—you danced only with me tonight. You walked with me, defended me—and when we have our lessons, you do things that I can only assume are intended to tempt me. And they succeed, Katrina. I am sorely tempted."

He moved in as if to kiss me, but the tip of his long nose poked my cheek. His fingers were cold and clammy around my upper arms, and his breath smelled musty as old books. I felt no physical desire for him at all. Ichabod appealed to my mind, while Brom's looks appealed to my body. Why, oh why could I not have *both* in one man?

"I need time." The words burst out more sharply than I intended.

Ichabod recoiled. "Then time you shall have, and space as well."

He clutched his book to his chest, as if to shield his heart from me.

"Ichabod—"

"I am sorry, Katrina—I need to be alone for a while."

He walked away, his thin shoulders hunched under that ridiculously large coat of his. Something about the sag of his posture pierced straight through my soul. I clenched my fists, threw back my head, and screeched with frustration. The night was black as ink, with a sprinkling of stars and a thin moon offering little light and even less hope for my situation.

Instead of trying to follow Ichabod or returning to the fire pit, I stalked back toward the house. The party was beginning to dissolve, with neighbors collecting their dishes and bidding my parents farewell. I was drawn into the farewells, too; and though I chafed at the performative niceties, I could do nothing but smile and nod until most of the guests had gone.

I could not get Ichabod's disappointment out of my head. Even if I did not wish to marry him, he was still my friend, a man I respected and liked. His pain twisted my heart, and I yearned to soften it, if I could manage to do so without giving him false hope. And I was worried, too, about his ability to manage the wicked old horse Gunpowder while he was in such a despondent state.

When I could get away from the farewells, I ran to the stables and asked Old Peter if Gunpowder was still in the stall. He shook his head. "The schoolmaster has just left, Miss Katrina. He was a sorry sight, trembling like aspen leaves. He could barely manage to mount his horse." Peter shook his head. "And that horse knew he was not fit to ride. The poor boy will likely be thrown before he reaches the bridge."

"Get me a horse, please, Peter," I told him.

"But—Miss Katrina—"

"Please." I laid my hand over his gnarled one. "I need to make sure that Ichabod gets home safely. If my parents ask where I am, tell them I am walking in the orchard with Brom. That will please them."

Peter nodded, resigned. "As you say, Miss Katrina."

He saddled my favorite horse, Nehalennia, and I mounted as best I could, hitching my party dress up to my thighs. Peter averted his eyes, his wrinkles deepening as he frowned. "Miss Katrina—"

"It's dark, Peter. No one will see."

I urged Nehalennia out of the yard and across the field, over the fence and along the road to the forest.

The instant my horse and I passed into the wood, the faint starlight and moonlight dimmed drastically. I could barely see the road, and my horse must have been navigating by sheer instinct and memory.

Crickets whistled a shrill chorus from the bushes, and fireflies winked on and off in the clearings as we passed. The smoky scent of the bonfires from home had drifted far over the valley and sifted between the branches, mingling with the damp, sweetish scent of rotting leaves. The cool breeze raised goosebumps along my arms, and I wished I had thought to bring a shawl.

I was nearly to the Old Church Bridge when I saw Ichabod's hat lying in the road, next to a smashed pumpkin.

My heart jolted, terror sending a fresh wave of goosebumps over my body. The tales of the Headless Horseman and the flaming pumpkin were still fresh in my mind.

With my heart throbbing in my throat, I dismounted and inched toward the broken pumpkin. Slowly I reached down to touch Ichabod's battered hat.

Hoofbeats vibrated through the earth, and I snapped upright, losing my grip on Nehalennia's reins.

Around the bend raced a man on horseback—I could not tell who it was, but at least I could distinguish the shape of a *head*. Thank goodness.

"Katrina?" Brom's voice. I was both relieved and disappointed. "I saw you leaving on horseback. What are you doing out here? It is not wise for a beautiful woman to be alone in the forest at night."

He swung off Daredevil and approached me. But instead of recapturing my horse's reins for me, he smacked Nehalennia's rump and sent her cantering away down the road, back toward home.

"Why did you do that?" I gasped.

He leaned in so close that his breath moved the stray curls around my face. "So you can ride back to the farm with me."

I drew back with a shaky laugh. "On Daredevil? I might fall."

"I will hold you tight." He smiled and moved closer, his nose brushing my cheek. "You are safe with me."

But I did not feel safe—not here, with no one else nearby, shrouded in shadows with Brom's enormous frame looming over me. There was something menacing and hungry about his stance and his expression, what little I could see of both in the gloom.

Again I backed away. "I need to find Ichabod. He was upset when he left, and still frightened from your terrible stories."

"Upset? Why was he upset?"

I winced, turning my back to him.

"Katrina." Brom's voice was both compulsion and threat at once. "Why was Ichabod Crane upset?"

"He offered me his hand in marriage, and I told him—"

"You refused him." Relief colors Brom's tone.

"No. I told him I would have to think about it."

Brom snorted. "What is there to think about?" He gripped my shoulders, shaking me slightly. "You and I have been meant for each other since we were young, Katrina. You know this is what our parents want—what *I* want. I will help you care for your father's holdings. My seed will yield healthy, strong children, not the spindly stalks you'll get from that scarecrow of a man. I am stronger than he is, more handsome, better liked—I have some wealth of my own, left by my father—I am the better match! Why do you hesitate? I offer my hand to you—take it!"

I jerked away. "You can keep your hand, and your *seed*. I am going to find Ichabod."

Brom snarled in frustration. "You drive me mad, Katrina. I know you want me—why else would you put your hands on me secretly?"

Ignoring him, I marched on down the road.

"At least ride with me to find the walking stick," Brom said. "Katrina! Come back here and ride."

But at that moment, Brom's horse, Daredevil, decided that he had waited long enough. A snort and a scuffle sounded behind me, and I turned just in time to see Daredevil half-rear, jerking the reins from Brom's hand before galloping back down the road, in the direction my mare took.

"The devil take you!" yelled Brom, stamping his boot impotently.

I snickered. "It seems your affinity for wild, difficult animals has finally backfired."

Brom strode up to me, grabbed my arm, and dragged me along the road toward the Old Church Bridge. "Let us find the spindly schoolmaster," he gritted between his teeth. "I have something I want to tell him."

We had not gone many steps when the treeline thinned, revealing the stone bridge bathed in silver moonlight. Unusually steep, it arched high over the stream, with yawning darkness beneath where the sun's long fingers never managed to touch. Besides its status as the particular haunt of the Horseman, the bridge was the subject of other tales. The goodwives whispered that trolls and wicked elves used to reside beneath the arch, tempting travelers to exchange their true names for beautiful gifts that later turned rotten and corrupt. When Lucas was but nine years old, he had ventured into the gloom under the bridge, on a dare. He swore ever afterwards that the very bank of the stream opened up to him that day, revealing a tunnel to Hell.

At the head of the bridge, just preparing to cross it, stood Ichabod.

"Ichabod!" Relief tinged my voice as I called to him. "Are you all right? We found a pumpkin on the road—and I thought maybe—you were—"

"Taken by the Horseman?" He turned to me, his thin face hard and bitter. "Your mother gave me a pie pumpkin to take home. But that devil Gunpowder bucked me off and trampled it. Nearly crushed me too, but I rolled out of the way just in time."

"And you were going to walk home in the dark, alone?"

Ichabod drew himself up to his full skinny height. "I am a grown man, Katrina. I am capable of walking home—and of *much more*."

"Ichabod, it's not that I think you aren't capable—"

Brom moved quick as a snake, striking Ichabod full in the face.

"Brom!" I shrieked.

"It's no more than he deserves for daring to think himself worthy of you," growled Brom. "I'll hit him again, to reinforce the lesson." He flexed his fingers and balled them into a fist once more.

"Brom." I caught his arm. "Stop."

"No, Katrina! He needs to know his place—a scraggly scarecrow of a teacher, leeching off the good people of this valley. He is a parasite, an insect." Brom practically spat the words.

Ichabod touched his lip and stared at the glistening scarlet blood on the tip of his finger. He looked at me, betrayal shining cold and hollow in his pale eyes. "You played with me, Katrina," he said quietly. "You are a coquette and a tease."

Brom backhanded him. "You do not speak to her!" he roared. "You do not think of her, or touch her! She is mine!"

I turned, my eyes narrowing. If Brom had not already fallen in my esteem due to his treatment of Ichabod, those words would have taken him down. In that moment, any vestiges of regard I had for Brom vanished from my heart.

"You do not own me," I hissed at him. "No man does."

He stared at me as if I had struck him. "You are getting emotional, Katrina, as women often do. You should go home. It is improper for you to be out here with no chaperone. Leave us."

I darted a look at Ichabod, who stood shivering yet defiant, his narrow shoulders lost in the fine greatcoat.

"You will walk me home, Brom. Come. I cannot go alone." I tugged at his sleeve, but he shook me off and shoved me away so roughly I staggered backward into the underbrush near the head of the bridge. Something sharp pierced my back, near my spine, and I cried out. When I moved forward, I felt the sharp thing retract from my body with a sucking, sickening pop.

"How dare you hurt her?" Ichabod charged at Brom, swinging wildly. Brom caught both Ichabod's fists in his own huge hands and marched the schoolmaster backward, onto the bridge.

"Stop!" Tears pooled in my eyes, both from the pain near my spine and from the fear that they would do each other a permanent harm. "Please stop!"

I reached around to my back, fingers trembling, and felt the stickiness of blood under the curve of my ribs. "Brom," I said faintly. "I have hurt myself, I think."

But he was too busy grappling with Ichabod to take notice of me. He gripped the schoolmaster by the coat collar, shaking him like a wayward pup. Then Brom threw him to the ground, and kicked him—kicked him again and again, furiously.

"Brom!" I screamed, sobbing. I turned, locating the sharp branch I had stumbled into. I wrenched and cracked it free of the trunk, driven by some vague notion of striking Brom over the head with it so he would stop beating Ichabod. With the pointed branch in both hands, I stumbled forward, gritting my teeth against the pain flooding my back and side.

Brom hauled Ichabod to his feet again and, with the force of a gale wind, he slung the schoolmaster along the length of the bridge.

Ichabod's skinny body hurtled toward me, collapsing against the spike in my hands—and there he stuck, pierced through the neck.

I froze, staring at the schoolmaster's head, thrown back, with the horrible blood-slicked spike of wood protruding from the front of his throat. More blood bubbled around the branch, glimmering darkly wet in the moonlight, splashing down onto the stones of the bridge. Ichabod's arms and legs flopped limp, like a scarecrow's.

My heart lurched, yearning to scream, but my voice would not work.

Every muscle in my body was frozen in place; I could not force my fingers to uncurl from the branch I held.

Brom stood paralyzed on the bridge, but he recovered faster than I.

"Katrina, you killed him," he said hoarsely.

"I—I was only trying to—"

"You killed the schoolmaster, Katrina."

Words spilled out of me, frantic and fast. "But you threw him at me. You were beating him, kicking him—I was going to help him."

"You would have struck me, Katrina? Me? You and I have been destined for a life together since we could toddle across the green." Brom advanced toward me. "Drop the stick."

My hands unclenched, and as Ichabod's body fell, Brom caught it and heaved it over the side of the bridge. "There. He fell on his way home, and that's an end of it. Maybe that foul devil of a horse threw him. You and I were never here."

"But Brom—we should everyone tell the truth." I shook my head, trying to dispel the dizziness that clouded my thoughts. "At least I am going to tell my father what happened. His death was an accident, but you—you beat him. That was wrong—"

Brom rushed forward, catching my throat in his hand. The vehemence of his words flecked my face with his spit. "You will say nothing. The schoolmaster was thrown by his horse, speared by a stray branch that he fell onto when he tumbled from the bridge. A terrible accident."

I squirmed in his grasp, trying to suck air through my compressed throat. "Brom—"

"Katrina." He swept a broad palm over my hair, dragged his knuckles down my cheek as I strained for breath. His mouth collided with mine, bruising my lips against my teeth. His grip loosened so I could breathe a little through my nose, but the assault on my mouth did not stop. Brom pushed me against the stone balustrade of the bridge, and the pressure against my wounded back made me whimper. He took it as encouragement and moved one hand to my chest, stroking and squeezing.

A cold wind rushed along the road. It rattled the black twigs and sent a flurry of crunchy brown leaves racing past my feet.

Hooves drummed faintly on packed dirt, ringing sharply against stone once or twice.

A wicked laugh echoed somewhere in the trees beyond the bridge—and then again, from the opposite side. I could have sworn I saw an orange star, or a lantern, or an amber will-o-wisp darting through the moon-silvered boughs of the trees.

Brom shoved himself away from me, nearly knocking me over the side of the bridge in the process. "Ho there! Who is it? Show yourself!"

Another trickle of inhuman laughter was his only answer—and the hoofbeats were growing louder.

"Come, Katrina. We cannot be caught here." He grabbed my hand. "We must run."

"I cannot run," I gasped. The edges of my vision darkened. The wetness on the back of my dress was spreading. "Brom, I am hurt."

He darted a panicked look down the road, where a shadow on horseback took shape in the gloom—a burly silhouette of inky black against the spiderweb of dark forest. There was something wrong about the silhouette, something missing. Broad shoulders, and between them a space—an emptiness. I squinted, sure that the oncoming rider must be slouching, hunched forward.

"The Headless Horseman," Brom breathed.

"No, that's a fireside tale," I whispered.

"If you cannot run, then hide!" Brom lurched away from me and pelted along the road in the direction of my house.

I clung to the low stony wall of the bridge, bowed over with pain and terror. "Brom, please. Do not leave me!" My call was barely audible over the rumble of hooves. I hated myself for trying to summon him back; but the devil I knew must be less dangerous than the headless one riding out of the night.

My legs would not hold me anymore. I sank against the side of the bridge, the stones scraping my back. I tried to reach around, tried to press the wound with my fingers to stop the seeping blood, but my strength was ebbing fast. I half lay by the wall, staring down at the moss-crusted flagstones of the bridge, staring at my fingers splayed across them—fingers splattered with Ichabod's blood and smeared with my own.

The pounding of the hooves slowed to a heartbeat's pace. When the first hoof struck the bridge, its iron shoe rang through the stones and reverberated into my very bones.

Another ringing step, and another.

My breaths came shallow and frenzied, mere sips of air, not enough to sustain life for long. But I could not face my death cowering against the stones. I must see the form of the man who was coming for my head.

Swallowing my terror, I turned, angling my face upward.

Knobby columns of black rose beside me—the horse's legs—and a giant body gleamed ebony and silver in the starlight. The horse snorted and shook its great head, its mane shimmering fluidly.

My gaze traveled to a massive leather boot, up a long muscled leg in tight dark trousers, to a heavy greatcoat topped with a wide collar, and—

No head.

I was expecting the head to be absent, but the sight of such strangeness, such wrongness, sent a jolt through my body.

The Horseman sat unmoving on his mount. Could he even see me as I cowered in the shadow of the wall? After all, he had no eyes.

An orange bolt streaked through the night—not a lantern or a star, but a ball of fire, with dark holes streaming flame and smoke. A skull—*his* skull. It hovered above the collar of his coat in wicked imitation of the head he had lost long ago.

And the skull, grinning and flickering with flame, angled its smoke-seared eye sockets toward me.

He saw me then. No hope of staying hidden until he passed.

My only chance—to beg his mercy.

"Hessian." My voice scraped raw through my throat. "I am no soldier as you once were, but I have seen an innocent man die tonight, and I am wounded. I beg you to spare me so I may seek justice for the schoolmaster, Ichabod Crane. If you look under the bridge, you can see his body. Please—help me—"

The Horseman's other hand, the one hidden behind the neck of his steed, rose slowly into my view. He gripped a viciously curved scythe that seemed to gleam with its own golden light. Was it made entirely of gold?

I could have sworn so—or perhaps I was finally yielding to the loss of blood, sinking into shadow.

I crumpled forward, prone on the flagstones, utterly spent. My eyelids fell shut, agony and a sinking heaviness taking me down into the dark.

The last thing I heard was a faint thud, and the scrape of boots on stone.

2

My consciousness resurfaced as I was dumped ungraciously onto a cloth-covered surface—a bed, maybe? I lay on my stomach, my face half-buried in something soft. Blinking, I tried to lift my head. But I caught only a hazy glimpse of a lantern, a table, and a chair before someone swore foully and wrapped a strip of cloth across my eyes. I squealed and tried to wrench away, but skilled fingers had the knot of the blindfold fastened before I could dislodge it.

"Be still," growled the voice—a male voice, rough as the stone of the bridge, and deep as a well. "Or I will cut off your head after all. Or perhaps you will bleed out, and save me the trouble."

There was a twist in the voice at the end of that sentence—humor, maybe? Dark humor, if so. His threat fixed me in place, still as a log—until the hands that had fixed my blindfold seized the back of my dress, and a cold blade grazed the nape of my neck. I screamed, but the hands took no notice. With a sharp rip of fabric, the man split my dress down the back and laid it open. Then he slit my shift and pushed that aside as well.

Warm air ghosted across my exposed skin, from the nape of my neck all the way to the base of my spine.

Breathless and blind, I waited, my nerves tingling.

The pads of work-worn fingers scraped along the tender flesh near my wound. My entire skin shivered at the contact and exploded into tiny bumps.

"Calm yourself," said the male voice. "I am checking the wound."

"Who are you?"

The fingers prodded my flesh, and with a pinch of pain something slid out of me—a splinter of the branch that had impaled me, perhaps.

"Take me home," I whispered. "Please."

"If I took you home now, you would die on the way. You have lost too much blood, too quickly. You need to be still and rest. Do not exert yourself, or I will have to tie you to the bed."

The image of myself bound to the bed face-down, helpless and exposed, should have terrified me. It did terrify me. It did *not* send a subtle thrill through my heart, because that would be foolish, and strange, and dreadfully inappropriate for the situation.

A cool, damp blob squished across the wound, mopping up blood.

"I need to sew this gash shut. Can you endure pain?"

"I can." I clenched my jaw in an agony of dread.

"Relax until I give you warning. I must heat water first, to cleanse the needle."

"Are you a physician then?" Maybe the Horseman had passed me by, and a traveling doctor had found me. Maybe the Horseman brought me to a physician—but this man did not sound like Dr. Burton, the only physician in Sleepy Hollow.

"I studied medicine a while," answered the voice. "In fact, I returned here to serve those who cannot afford proper care for their health."

My interest in the man redoubled, but I could not ask more questions, not when my insides were afire with pain and my muscles felt weak and watery. With my eyes forced shut under the blindfold, I began to slip into unconsciousness again.

The man's voice spoke close by. "I will begin now."

Something pierced the muscle of my back, a sharp dot of pain. I whimpered and squeezed my eyes shut even tighter. Another stab of pain, and another, and another. The skin around my wound pulled dreadfully, and I brought my knuckle up to my mouth and bit it hard.

"That part is done," the voice assured me.

He smeared a cool paste across the area, and a dry cloth dropped into place over that. His hands slid along my waist, between my skin and my dress, passing a bandage around me and tying it snugly.

Sometime during the wrapping of the bandage, a tingling warmth began low in my belly, woken by the skim of calloused palms over my body. Being touched by this stranger, being exposed to him—it excited me in a way I did not expect—especially when, during his ministrations, his fingertips brushed the center of my lower back. The feeling that awakened was subtle, rendered distant by pain and weariness—but it was there nonetheless.

"Lie still," the man said, with a final pat to the bandage. From what I could hear, it sounded as though he was gathering up his supplies, putting them away.

He did not fold my dress back together over my bare skin, probably because the back of the gown was soaked with my blood.

"I cannot lie still," I fretted. "Not until you tell me who you are, and why you brought me here."

"You asked me for help."

Fear thickened in my throat, dispelling the warmth I felt a moment ago. Only one person—one Thing—had been with me on the bridge after Brom left. "So then—you are—"

"Yes, tell me who I am, farm girl." His voice dripped with an unmistakable sneer.

It sounded ridiculous to say it aloud. "The Headless Horseman," I murmured. "The Hessian soldier from ages ago—"

"That is horse-shit," he snapped. "I am twenty-four years old. I have not been alive long enough be that damned Hessian. I am not Hessian at all."

Listening more closely to the cadence of his voice, I caught a lilting accent, faint but discernible. "You are of Irish ancestry, then."

Silence.

"How are you talking to me if you have no head?" I pictured a flaming skull floating bodiless near me, speaking on behalf of the torso that was binding my wound. The image drove spikes of anxious pain deep into my stomach.

"I have a head. Stop asking questions."

"I will stop asking questions when you stop answering them. How does your head go back on, then? Or did you—did you borrow Ichabod's head?" The question conjured a mental image more fearsome than the first.

"You know nothing about any of this. Keep your mouth shut, or I will stuff it with something."

"With what?"

"I—I do not know—a cloth, or something. Maybe a potato."

"How about a carrot? Do you have any of those?"

A few seconds of stunned silence, and then he said tightly, "Do you have any idea what you are saying, or do words simply spill out of your mouth?"

"I am hungry, and if I am to be stuffed with vegetables, I would prefer a raw carrot to a raw potato."

The Horseman made a choking sound, almost as if he smothered a laugh. "I suppose you should eat something. You lost a lot of blood. Not as much as the poor fellow under the bridge, though. I need to go and clean that up."

"Clean it up?"

"I must move the body. If he stays where he is, I may be discovered. I will bury him and wash the blood from the bridge. Everyone will think he left for another teaching post in some distant village. Or they will attribute his disappearance to a darker entity." The dull thunk of a bucket reached my ears as he spoke. "Stay here, and do not move. Try to sleep. When I return, I will get you something to eat."

My fingers twitched, eager to remove the blindfold as soon as he left; but he must have noticed the movement, because a second later he caught my wrist and wound it with thin rope, knotting it tight. My arm jerked upward as he tugged the rope, lashing it to something else—the bedpost, maybe.

"I cannot allow you to look around freely, or to kill yourself in some misguided attempt to run home." He grabbed my other wrist and fastened it the same way. I would have fought, but weakness flooded my body. The bit of energy I had summoned in order to question him drained away, leaving exhaustion behind.

"Sleep," he said. "I will return soon."

With my back speared by repeated flares of pain, and my hands bound, and my eyes covered, I had no choice but to drift off to sleep.

A harsh bang jarred me awake, and I writhed, confused and panic-stricken, gasping in terror.

"Hush! Hush now." A warm palm pressed between my bare shoulder blades. "You are safe."

"Safe." I burst into shrill laughter. "Safe, blindfolded and bound, in the haunt of the Headless Horseman. Yes, I feel very safe."

"Haunt?"

"Yes. Ghosts have haunts, places they haunt—or perhaps we are in hell after all."

"Does this feel like hell to you?"

The pressure of his hand on my back felt suddenly too heavy, too intimate. I could smell him—sour sweat and bitter smoke.

I wrinkled my nose. "It smells like hell."

His hand disappeared from my skin. "I am cut to the quick that you disapprove of my *smell*. I have been occupied in washing blood from the bridge. Do you know how many bucketfuls of water it took? While you lay here at your leisure—"

"My leisure? You take me from the road and bind my wound, then you truss me up like a prisoner." I tugged against the bonds, but I was too weak from hunger to pull very hard.

"Shall I let you stagger home hungry and half-naked amongst the wolves and wanderers? I care not what they will do to you. But I doubt they will smell any better than I do."

"They cannot smell much worse," I retorted through clenched teeth.

"Would your ladyship rather I bathe first, and then feed you? My stench might turn your appetite."

My stomach twisted with hunger at the thought of having to wait longer for food. "No, no—please. I need food now."

"Hm. I think not. I think I shall draw water, and heat it, and luxuriate in the bath awhile. And then we will see about your meal."

I groaned, lurching against the bonds, but when the wound pained me sharply, I quieted again. "At least remove the blindfold."

"I cannot let you see me, or your surroundings. I cannot trust you not to tell anyone about me, or my haunt, as you call it. If you should glimpse my face, or see where you are, why then—I would have to take measures to protect myself."

My breath quickened. Would he kill me to hide his identity?

"I would rather not see your face anyway," I said. And because I could not resist— "You are probably hideous in both face and form."

A chuckle rumbled from him. "You wish that were true."

His scent and his presence vanished, and I heard the clanking of a pot as he prepared to heat the water.

"If you were handsome I would have seen you around, and I would recognize your voice," I threw at him. "All the most handsome young men in this valley and beyond come to court me."

"Is that so?"

"It is."

"And why is that?"

"Because I am beautiful, rich, and accomplished. And I am pleasant to be with. Good company."

"Good company?" he snorted. "You are nearly as unpleasant as I am—perhaps more so, because of all the whining, and the questions."

"You are nothing but a fiend. An unholy demon of darkness, who committed some vile original sin and was condemned to an equally horrible fate."

Something squeaked—a door? His voice traveled to me from the vicinity of the sound, and its depth and timbre sent a shiver through my body. "And what sin do you think me guilty of?"

"Murder? Greed? Envy?" I swallowed. "Lust?"

"I am guilty on all counts. But none of those sins caused my condition. I was born into this curse, and I will die with it."

The door slammed.

He went in and out several more times, carrying the water for his bath, but I did not speak to him again. My mind raced with possibilities. His corporeal nature ruled out a ghost or spirit, though it did not eliminate the possibility of his being a demon. But since when did demons sweat, and bathe, and stitch up a human's wounds?

Lying on my belly, with my wrists still bound, I could not remove the blindfold; but it seemed to have loosened a little. Maybe I could shift it by rubbing my face against the pillow. I desperately wanted a glimpse of him, though he might kill me for it.

The splash and hiss of water told me that he was nearly done preparing the bath. Firmly I rubbed my cheek and temple against the pillow, scraping the blindfold gradually until it inched up a fraction, allowing me a narrow slit of visibility from my left eye.

First I saw an expanse of thickly-muscled back, a sweep of powerful shoulders, a massive neck holding up—thank God—a *head* of close-cropped black hair. A wide band of gold circled the Horseman's throat. There seemed to be faint markings on it, but I could not tell for sure at this distance, with my limited field of vision.

Then my gaze drifted from the golden collar, down that naked back, to the beautifully curved rump and strong legs of the Horseman.

He stepped into the round wooden tub and sank down with a sigh of relief. With his nakedness partially hidden from me, I remembered the necessity of breathing occasionally. My face burned with shameful delight at what I had just seen.

The tub he had filled was not very large; he had to fold his legs up to his chest to fit into it, and he kept shifting his body to get comfortable. After a few minutes he began passing a bar of soap over himself, leaving a glistening trail of iridescent bubbles across his tanned skin.

Reluctantly I shifted my gaze to the room. I could not see much of it—a fireplace, table, chair, the tub—a bundle of herbs hanging against the wall. All commonplace items, but nothing that triggered a memory or familiarity. Yet he must be somewhat known to the people in the valley, or he would not be so concerned about me recognizing and revealing him.

The Horseman stood up in the tub, water trailing from his body in sheets and droplets. With his back toward me, he began to wash his—nether regions.

I shut my eye tight. And then I opened it again.

The swelling, tingling warmth returned to my body, centering between my thighs. I knew what it was—I had felt it before, when I was teasing Brom or Ichabod. I had indulged those sensations when I was alone at night, in my room. But somehow the private sessions were never entirely satisfying. After a brief ripple of pleasure, I was always left lacking, wanting.

The Horseman sank into the water again, rinsing away the soap and then using a bucket to lather and rinse his hair. With his back toward me, he climbed out of the tub, snatched a cloth, and began rubbing his body with it.

Good Lord in Heaven. This was a sweet torture beyond anything I had ever felt.

He began to turn around.

Quickly I scraped my face against the pillow, shifting my blindfold back into place.

"You are very quiet," he said. "But your breathing is quick, so you are not asleep. How do you feel?" His bare feet scuffed the wooden floor, and his wrist pressed to my forehead. "No fever yet. Good."

"I am fine," I managed. "A little pain—and—hunger."

"I will get you something to eat." A scuffle of cloth over skin as he dressed himself. A scraping of dishes and utensils. Then he undid the knots around my wrists. "Keep your blindfold on if you value your life."

"You would kill me, after saving me?" My lips curved in a disbelieving smile.

"Not of my own free will. But I might be made to do so."

"*Made* to do so?"

He sighed. "I'm going to help you sit up, slowly. We must be very careful or your stitches will burst. Do you understand?"

"Yes." Questions burned in my mind, but they could wait until after food.

With the Horseman's hands supporting me, I managed to sit up, slowly and painfully. And then I became aware of another need, more pressing than hunger. "Do you have a privy? An outhouse?"

Another sigh. "You should not walk that far. I will bring you a bedpan."

"I cannot use a bedpan with all these skirts!"

"Then you should take them off."

My jaw dropped. I could take off the outer gown and keep my shift on, but the back of it was cut apart, ruined, and stiff with my dried blood. The shift would likely fall off if I moved too quickly—not that I planned to in my current weakened state.

"I will need something else to wear."

"I will find you something. Stand up," the Horseman ordered. "Hold on to me if you feel faint."

Rising to my feet sent waves of dizziness through my head, made worse by my lack of sight. I wavered and nearly fell. The Horseman caught me, swearing again. The growl of those foul words, right by my ear, nearly overwhelmed me. I fumbled for support, my fingers traveling across his chest to his arm.

"I will take the dress off for you, if you will permit me," he said. "We must hurry. You should not be on your feet for long."

I nodded my permission, clutching his shoulder while he worked my gown off my shoulders and downward. After some more wrestling and swearing on his part, I was able to step out of all the skirts and petticoats. The only bit of material left was my shift, and the simple drawers I had stitched for myself. Most women did not wear drawers unless it was their time of bleeding, or unless they were temptresses—but I preferred the undergarments. They made me feel secretly scandalous.

Only now, they were a barrier to what I needed to do. I could not bend over to remove them without reopening my wound.

"I will fetch the bedpan and some clothing," said the Horseman. "Sit down until I return."

While he was gone I fretted over my choices. Either preserve some modesty and remove the drawers myself, even if doing so opened my stitches—or brazenly ask this strange man to remove them for me.

He seemed respectable enough. He had not touched me beyond what was necessary for my physical health. But I had been taught that a woman's body was an irresistible invitation to sin, and that a man could not be blamed for what happened next if a woman should take the temptation too far.

The Horseman's steps returned, and something metal clanked to the floor by the bed. "There. The pan is near your feet, and there is a spare tunic of mine on the bed beside you. Put it on with the laces at the back instead of the front, so I can check your wound when I need to. I will leave you to it."

"Wait!" I reached out blindly, but missed his arm. "I need your help with one more thing. I am wearing drawers, and I don't think I can remove them without undoing your good work on my wound."

"Ah." He cleared his throat. "Very well." Something scrapes across the floor. "Here is a chair. Stand up and hold onto it so you do not fall over."

I obeyed him, trying not to tremble as his hands slid quickly under my shift, all the way up to my hips, and then down again.

"Lift your foot. Now the other. Good. I will return in a few moments. If you need me, call out."

"What should I call you?"

"What do you mean?"

"Should I call you 'Horseman'? You have a name, surely?"

"Not one I am stupid enough to give you."

"But I will give you mine. I am Katrina Van Tassel, only daughter of Baltus Van Tassel." I waited for his response. When he did not reply, I urged, "You have heard of my family, yes?"

"Yes."

"And?"

"And I know that you are a shameless coquette who plays men against each other—a game which apparently results in death."

Until now, my situation had distracted me. I had not let myself think for more than a second about Ichabod. But at the Horseman's words, a wave of grief crashed over me.

"It was an accident," I whispered, clutching the chair for support. "And I did not play them against each other on purpose—they did most of it themselves. What is a woman to do when so many men want her and she wants none of them?"

"None of them? You must be very difficult to please."

"Perhaps." Tears oozed from beneath my lashes, soaking the blindfold. "Perhaps it is all my fault that a woman's youth and beauty turns men into idiots. All my fault that I was expected to select either the foolish schoolteacher who loved my land or the boorish rake who loved my body. Perhaps it was my fault that when I tried to comfort one of them, the other decided to beat him senseless. My fault, too, that the same ill-fated branch that harmed me should be the accidental cause of a good man's death. You are right. I am *very* difficult to please, and everything is my fault. Now if you will leave the room, perhaps I can at least relieve myself and change clothes with a little dignity."

With a shuffle of chastened steps, the Horseman left the room.

I took care of my needs first. Then I shrugged out of the shift and slid the Horseman's tunic over my head. It was made of cotton, worn soft, and it smelled of fresh soil and mountain streams and lye soap. Unlaced and worn backwards, it was very loose around the neck, and kept sliding off my shoulder, while the hem fell nearly to my knees. Without trying to put on the drawers, I eased myself back onto the bed, lying carefully on my left side.

Should I stay in this bed and recover, or try to leave? I did not think the Horseman would stop me if I truly wished to go home, but I could not be sure. The dizziness in my head and the weak tremor of my muscles made my decision for me, at least for the moment. My body had been through terror and trauma, and I must give it time.

Soon the Horseman returned, collected the pan and the bloodied clothes, and carried them away. When he came back, he dragged the chair close to my bedside. "Sit up a little, so you do not choke on your food. And open your mouth."

With no strength left to question or wonder, I propped myself on one elbow; and although my wound tugged, it did not hurt too badly in that position. I opened my lips, and he set a cup against them and helped me drink. When I pulled away, he pressed me to take the rest of the water. "Keeping the body filled with liquids is a vital part of healing."

Once I had drunk all the water, he placed a morsel of bread and soft cheese on my tongue. When the Horseman gave me the next bite, my lips brushed over his thick fingers. He jerked his hand away so fast I barely got the morsel of food.

"You do not have to feed me," I said. "I can eat it myself."

He shoved something onto the bed beside me and plopped my hand onto it. My fingertips wandered over rough bread, squishy cheese, and strips of something cold—possibly ham. "Feed yourself. I need to sleep anyway."

Of course. He hadn't slept all night.

"Where will you sleep?" This room seemed to serve multiple purposes—I wasn't sure if he had another bedroom or not.

"On the floor," he answered. "Now hush."

"What is to stop me from taking off my blindfold while you sleep?"

"Your desire to keep your head on your shoulders. If you saw my face, even if you did not recognize me yourself, you could describe me to others. Or you might encounter me in town and let slip who I am."

His words brought to life a dozen or more questions in my mind. Slowly I chewed, ranking the questions by order of importance. This man, with the careful hands and the deep voice—could he really be the terrifying Horseman, the one whom every soul in Sleepy Hollow feared?

"How many have you killed?" I asked.

"That is a cruel question."

"You cut off people's heads. I think it is a *fair* question."

"I have taken seven heads in my twenty-four years."

"Why?"

"Put some bread in your mouth, I beg you," he groaned. "Why the devil didn't I leave you on that bridge?"

I decided not to press the matter until I had eaten and he had slept. While I ate, I heard him arranging something on the floor—probably some blankets. After a while there was no more sound, save for his slow, deep breathing.

When I finished my meal, I thought about taking the blindfold off. I could peek, just once, and he would never know. But a crawling dread in the back of my mind prevented me from yielding to the impulse. Did I really want to know what he looked like? Did I want to risk his wrath? He had hinted that he was not completely in control of himself when it came to his victims. Was that merely an excuse? Or perhaps someone or something else was controlling him, some demon, spirit, or ghost. In that case, the mysterious entity might be able to perceive me, to know if I removed my blindfold or not.

Weariness weighed my head and limbs again. I took the plate and reached it downward, over the edge of the bed, until I felt it touch the floorboards. Then I resumed my position on my left side and let myself float away into sleep.

3

Still half-swimming in sleep, I sensed something brushing my upper arm. Fingers, warm and rough.

My right breast felt strangely bare, the cool air of the room teasing it to a hard peak.

Was the Horseman removing my clothes?

I lashed out with a fist and by sheer luck caught him square in the throat, one of my knuckles knocking against the collar he wore. He choked a protest but continued the movement of his hand—tugging the loose tunic back *up*, over my shoulder.

"Your shirt slipped down as you slept!" he said. "I am only trying to cover you."

"So throw a blanket over me," I snapped. "Do not touch me."

"Foolish, vain girl," he growled. "Do you think I wanted to touch you? I would much rather be left alone."

"Then I will go." I lurched upright, biting back a cry at the flare of pain. "Point me to the front door, show me the road home—I will travel it. I do not care if my wound opens again. Anything is better than this strange place, and you." I threw as much venom as I could muster into the words.

"No one can know you were here." Distress tinged his voice. "It could be dangerous."

"Because the people of the valley might come after you with muskets and fire?"

"No, fool. Dangerous for *you*. If my m—if the one who controls me learned of your presence here, you would not be safe."

I halted, wavering on my feet, clinging to the bedpost. It was as I suspected, then. "The one who controls you? What does that mean?"

He groaned. "I cannot—I should not say—"

Canting my head to listen, I moved toward his voice. "But you will tell me. You must."

"Rest here one more day, and I will tell you what I can."

"Why? Why should I stay here any longer?"

"Because if you try to walk back down into the valley, you will die. You nearly bled out on that bridge, Katrina."

Katrina. The way his deep voice flowed around the syllables of my name was a delight I had not anticipated.

In addition to the gift of my name on his tongue, he had given me a clue about our location. He said, if I tried to walk back down into the valley, I would die—so we were somewhere in the hills above Sleepy Hollow. Several families—woodcutters, trappers, and such—resided in the hills. Mentally I ran through the few names I could remember, but I knew I was missing some of them. The hill folk tended to be reclusive, visiting the floor of the valley only to sell their goods and fetch supplies, or to attend the occasional holiday frolic.

I kept moving in the direction that I last heard his voice. The stitches on my back tugged painfully with every step. "Were you truly trying to cover me, to preserve my modesty?"

"Yes."

"Why should I believe you?"

"Because I could have stripped you naked at any time since I brought you here." He caught my outstretched hands at the wrists. His own hands were massive, warm, and strong—their heat slithered along my arms to my heart.

"You are too weak to resist me," he said quietly. "It would be easy to take what I want."

"Too weak to resist you?" I forced out the words, willing my voice not to tremble. "Do I need to hit you again, to prove my strength?"

He laughed. "No need."

I moved closer, until my legs touched something—his knees maybe? Was he sitting in the chair near my bed? "You said, 'take what I want.' Does that mean you *do* want me?"

"Get back in bed, Katrina."

I wanted to rip aside the blindfold, to turn the full power of my eyes on him, to see if I could entrance him the way I did so many others—but I settled for a coy smile. As I slipped my wrists from his grip, I trailed the tips of my fingers across his palms. I thought I heard a faint sigh from him.

The bed felt so comfortable I could not suppress a groan of relief as I sank back onto it. Still, anxiety clouded my comfort. "I cannot stay here another day. What will my family think of my disappearance?"

"When you return, simply tell them that you were attacked by the Horseman. Tell them that a woodcutter and his wife rescued you and nursed you back to health, but they would not tell you their names because they did not want your family to feel beholden or to offer recompense—and because they did not want the Horseman to wreak vengeance on them for stealing away his prize."

It was a good plan. My parents would likely believe it. I nodded my acceptance and fumbled around on the bed for a blanket. No sooner had I found one than he snatched it away and whipped it out, letting it drift down over me.

"I will need to check your wound later," said the Horseman. "For now, rest."

"Your favorite word—rest," I mumbled. "I am not used to so much resting."

"No? I thought the Van Tassel heiress would have little to do."

"I make things to do. I help with the work, I ride, I study music, I read, and I fish—"

"You fish?"

"Shocking, I know. I usually have to smuggle the fish to one of the boys on my father's farm, so he can claim that he caught them. My parents have no idea how many of the finely dressed fish on their table came from my line."

"What other shocking things do you enjoy?"

Tension gripped the silence after his words. I could not helping grinning even as I blushed.

"I only meant—I was curious—" The Horseman was *stammering*. Flustered. Embarrassed. My heart swelled with delight at the realization.

"I know what you meant," I replied. "Let's see—I sew myself fine undergarments, as you know. Very scandalous. I sometimes make up stories in my head during the parson's sermons—the wildest and wickedest tales—you would blush and faint if you heard them. I also whittle on occasion—I have a collection of tiny figures that I have made, and the scars to show for it." I held up my hands, indicating the inner flesh of my left thumb. I knew the scars intimately, though I could not see them. "See? I stabbed myself just there. And here, a fairly deep cut. Nearly sliced the pad off this finger—see the crescent-shaped mark? I also like to hunt for nests in the forest. I take the prettiest empty eggshells, if I can find those that are mostly intact—and I paste them back together, thread them on string, and hang them above the fireplaces at home. They make the loveliest decorations. Although I suppose that isn't very shocking, especially not to a man who occasionally loses his head."

He did not answer.

"The collar you wear has something to do with it." My words weren't a question, but a statement. "I saw markings along it—perhaps a spell of some kind. Ichabod Crane—the schoolmaster, the man you buried—he told me of such things. He had a theory that you were some Celtic creature of myth—a dull-man? Dulligan? Dull—"

"Dullahan." The Horseman's tone lent the word a dark flavor.

I seized the word eagerly. "Dullahan. Yes. Ichabod said you could be human sometimes, and at other times—not. He also said something about dullahan being 'summoned' for direful deeds."

"Damn, I had no idea he knew so much. No wonder—" The Horseman cut himself off short.

"What?" My fists gripped bunches of the blanket as I waited, hanging on his every word.

"I will tell you the truth," he said. "I was sent out that night to kill your schoolmaster, Ichabod Crane."

My breath hitched. "He was not *my* schoolmaster."

"But you cared about him."

"I did. He was a friend. He and Brom—they were both my friends." Tears pressed at the backs of my covered eyelids. "Why would anyone want him dead?

He could be silly sometimes, yes—a little avaricious and foolish—but he never hurt anyone—"

But he did, after all. My mind flashed to a memory—I had been walking by the schoolhouse one bright morning when I heard the most heart-breaking wails and sobs. I hurried round the corner and there was Ichabod, with a switch poised to strike the thighs of a skinny schoolboy.

"Ichabod!" I had shouted.

He turned, shocked at my tone.

"Why are you beating this boy?"

"He will not stop moving during classes," Ichabod had said through gritted teeth. "He is constantly jiggling his knees, and wiggling around, and squirming, and asking questions—"

"As an intelligent boy *should* do," I retorted. "Perhaps he is bored of the lesson. Perhaps he needs more stimulating material to study."

Ichabod's face had flushed red under my criticism. "Perhaps you should leave the instruction of the urchins to me, Miss Katrina, and return to your promenade."

"Only if you spare him this once."

Ichabod had reluctantly agreed, and I had kept walking. But afterward I wondered how many other times he had beaten those little children for their need to move, and to question, and to *be*.

Ichabod had hurt people. Small people, yes—but people nonetheless. Perhaps that was no reason for him to die horribly as he did—but I could not continue declaiming his innocence. In his own way, Ichabod could be as merciless as Brom.

The Horseman spoke quietly. "Guilty of harm or not—it was his knowledge of the dullahan that led to his destruction, I think. That, and one other reason."

"And I suppose this 'other reason' cannot be revealed?" I pushed out my lower lip in a pout that usually got me whatever I wanted.

Apparently the Horseman was immune to my lips and their charms. "I cannot say more."

"This is completely ridiculous," I snapped. "You dribble out bits of information but you will say nothing clearly. You provide no comprehensive information."

"I understand your frustration." His voice sounded nearer than I expected—I thought I felt the puff of his breath against my hair. "But aren't you being rather unreasonable, expecting the Headless Horseman of Sleepy Hollow to spill all his secrets to you?"

"You owe me the truth."

"And why is that?"

I could sense him—very close to me now, a tingling heat charging the air between us. "Because—well, because—"

"It is you who owe me, for tending to you, for lending you a bed and shelter, for giving you food and drink. Fortunately for you, I am a magnanimous monster and will require no repayment. Now, if you are not going back to sleep, allow me to check your wound."

I rolled from my side onto my stomach, scrunching the blanket in both hands, under my chin. The warm air of the room drifted soft across my exposed back as I waited, in an agony of anticipation, for the Horseman to touch me.

He spread the V-shaped opening at the back of the tunic, fussed with the bandage, then lifted it away. His fingers pressed lightly at the edge of the wound. "No infection. You seem to be healing well, and quickly. I will clean this and add more of the poultice, just to be safe. And a fresh bandage, of course. Be still."

"Yes, Lord Horseman."

His fingers paused. "What?"

"Lord Horseman. It suits you, I think. You would not give me your name."

"I'll be damned if I let you call me 'Lord Horseman.'"

"Perhaps I should choose another name—like Tom, or Hans. Oh, how about Absalom? I have always wanted to name my future child Absalom. Such a sensual name, don't you think? And the biblical character was rather wicked and tragic, which makes it all the better. Absalom suits you. Absalom you shall be, until you agree to tell me your true name."

"My *true name*?" He patted a cloth across my wound. "You sound like one of the Fae, demanding my name in that way."

A devilish impulse took root in my heart—or perhaps it had taken root long ago, and my next words were merely the natural offshoot of the nourishment I gave it.

I spoke in my silkiest tones. "I do want your name, and I will give you something in exchange for it."

"Is that so." The Horseman did not sound the least bit interested. He smoothed paste over the wound and placed another bandage. I sighed at the absence of his fingers on my skin.

"If you give me your name," I said, "I will let you touch me. Anywhere you like."

His shock quivered in the very air, nearly palpable. A gruff sound issued from his throat. "Now I know you are Fae, for that is a wicked bargain indeed. No chaste, god-fearing girl would say such a thing."

"I am not a *girl*," I snarled, forgetting my attempt to be charming. "I am a woman. And we have enough secrets between us already—why not another? One that we share, that we keep from everyone else?"

I lay still, awaiting his reply. My heart swelled and throbbed until I feared it might burst through my ribs and be revealed, raw and hot and pulsing.

"Why do you want me to touch you?"

"I—I want your name."

"But you could have placed any price on that knowledge. You chose this one. Why?"

"Because it's something you want," I snapped. "Do not deny it."

"And you think I am so crazed with desire that I will deliver you my name in exchange for the privilege of laying a hand on some private part of you?"

His hand—on some private part of me—oh heaven and hell. The space between my thighs grew warm and liquid, and a delicate ache slithered through my stomach.

"I—I don't know—"

"You seem distracted." His voice shifted deeper, velvety as a damp mossy hollow beside a stream, where violets grew fragrant and lush—

I reined in my thoughts abruptly. "I'm not distracted. I'm—frustrated."

His tone grew deeper still, with a breadth to the sound that told me he was smiling, damn him—"Frustrated? And why is that?"

"Because—because I want your name!"

"Hmm." He secured the bandage and tugged the blanket out of my fists, spreading it over me again. "So sad to see a woman in such distress. But Katrina, not every man melts for your sweet smiles—or yields to your sharp tongue."

"I will show you a sharp tongue," I muttered. "You have not felt its lash yet, fiend."

"Fiend? You called me that once already. I rather like it."

"Then I christen you Absalom, Fiend of Hell." My mouth twitched, but I was determined not to smile.

"You have given me a name, so I will allow you to touch *me*." And before I could speak a word, the Horseman caught my hand and pressed it to his cheek.

My breath jerked in my lungs, and my heartbeat pulsed wild in my throat. My palm scraped over rough stubble; my fingertips curled under the edge of a hard jawline. As my thumb swept across smooth, slanted cheekbone, its tip grazed a fringe of thick lashes. Hungry for more sensation, I shifted my hand, trailing my fingers across a pair of full, curved lips.

I drew in a jagged breath. "Good God. You are beautiful."

He pulled away, vanishing from my reach. "And you—you are—"

Beautiful. He would tell me I was beautiful too, and then—

"Annoying."

I frowned. "What?"

"I'll be back. Use the bedpan again if you need to." His footsteps clumped away again.

"What an insufferable ass!" I said loudly, hoping he would hear it. "Talking of bedpans at such a moment. I will kill him yet, if he does not kill me first."

But the words sobered me rather than soothing my anger. After all, being killed by the Horseman was still a very real possibility. With the Horseman absent, I could see my own peril more clearly. His magnetic presence, his voice, and his scent no longer muddled my thoughts.

I needed to get away from here. Back home, my bedroom waited for me, full of my own things—the quilt I'd had since childhood, the lace-edged pillowcases, the glossy milk-white porcelain bowl and pitcher on my washstand. My mother would bring me tea and pet my hair, and our cook, Annie, would surely make me something special to help me recover from my ordeal. Old Dr. Burton would inspect my wound and fuss over me. I would have books to read, fresh flowers to sketch, pastries to enjoy. My foolish fascination with the Horseman would be over, and I would be safe.

In a moment of frantic decision, I ripped off the blindfold. I used the bedpan quickly and then padded on bare feet to the heavy wooden door.

It stood slightly open, and for a moment I feared I might encounter the Horseman's baleful eye watching me through the crack. Cautiously I eased it wider, conscious of increasingly sharp flickers of pain along the seam the Horseman had sewn along my wound.

A dark hallway lay beyond the door. Along its right-hand wall, narrow shelves were stacked with goods. I squinted at them and noted bags of flour and meal, jars of preserves, clay pots, bundles of dried herbs, strings of onions, clumps of carrots, a pumpkin or two, and a lumpy sack, probably full of potatoes—or skulls.

Daylight seeped under a door at the far end of the hallway.

Desperation loosed my feet and I ran to the door, keeping my steps as light as I could. I seized the handle and pushed—but a horrific stab of pain shot through my back and bowels as I lurched into the white glare of the outdoors.

I nearly screamed. Spots swam in front of my eyes, and I braced my forehead against the rough log wall of the cabin, biting my fist in agony. The Horseman had said I nearly bled to death. Perhaps my wound went deeper than I realized.

My breath hissed in and out through my teeth. I risked a slow movement—again the pain shot across my lower back, and with it an oozing sensation. Did I tear open my stitches?

Eyes tightly closed against the pain, I tried to form rational thoughts.

I could try to keep going, to find a path down to the valley. But if a brief run down the hall and a lunge through the door had done such damage, a two or three hour walk would certainly do me in.

I could stagger back into the cabin and collapse on the bed again. I could tell the Horseman that I fell while using the bedpan, and that tore my stitches that way. He might believe me. Or he might realize that I defied him, and then he would refuse to help me anymore.

"Curse this godforsaken wound!" I struck my forehead against the log.

A large hand landed atop my head, holding it immobile. "I suggest you avoid damaging yourself further."

Every muscle in my body softened with relief, even as my blood chilled at the heavy disappointment in the Horseman's voice.

"Katrina." His mouth brushed my ear, and I could not help thinking of those soft, full lips I had touched. "Why did you disobey me?"

"I am afraid you might kill me," I replied, in a voice as sick and quivering as my stomach felt.

His hand tightened a little, slid downward toward my neck slowly, as if he was memorizing the shape of my skull. "I may have to. But I would rue the day."

"What does that mean? You have to tell me what's going on. Please. Ignorance does not keep anyone safe. It only augments the danger, and heightens anxiety."

"You may be right." He collected my hair into a fistful and gently tilted my head backward, just a little. I kept my eyes shut. "But should I reward such blatant disregard for your physician's orders?"

"Surely you can understand my reluctance to trust said physician."

"Yet you would beg for my touch."

"I did not beg! I would never do such a thing."

"Hm. Pity." The Horseman's fingertips brushed my waist, and he let loose a sharp swear. "You have torn your stitches, you insufferable fool! Inside, now."

He hitched my arm across his burly shoulders and we shuffled inside together, back to the room where he helped me onto the bed with a gentleness that belied the incessant stream of profanity from his mouth. Some of the curse words were new to me.

"I had heard that Irishmen were foul of speech," I told him as he replaced the blindfold over my eyes. "But you must have the foulest tongue of them all."

"Keep silent until I have repaired the damage you did," he snapped.

I waited until he was done stitching me up again, and then I said, "You really did save my life. And I'm not your prisoner, am I? You merely want me to stay here so I can heal."

"As I have told you. And only *now* you believe it?"

"How long must I stay?"

His sigh was a gust of frustration. "Two days if you behave, longer if you don't."

"Will you stay and talk to me?"

"I have work to do—gardening, trapping, cutting wood—I am no man of leisure."

"When your work is done, then?"

"Are you begging?"

"I—very well, yes. I am begging you to talk to me, and tell me about yourself, and about this curse under which you suffer."

His hesitation clouded the space between us as he secured fresh bandages. "I am not supposed to speak of it."

"Are you under a spell that keeps you silent on the topic?"

"Not exactly."

"Then tell me anyway." Desperately I scrambled for some reason why he should trust me. "If you have told no one before, you may find that telling another soul is a comfort. And I have no cause to babble your story to anyone else. As far as anyone will ever know, my time was passed in a woodcutter's cottage, under the pious care of his good wife. To speak any other truth would be to condemn myself to a lifetime of gossip and censure."

"True. Any connection with someone like me would certainly be an ill-advised thing." His steps clumped toward the door, scuffing a little slower than usual.

"That is not what I meant—I—Horseman? Absalom? Sir Fiend?"

But if he heard me, he made no response or return.

I lay for hours alone, dozing fitfully. When the Horseman returned with a great thumping and banging, I startled awake with a yelp.

"You take fright easily," he said. "It is only me."

I wished he would lay his palm against my back again to reassure me, but tension laced his tone and I knew better than to push my luck. Strange how I was beginning to know the colors and cadence of his voice.

A chair dragged to my beside and creaked as he settled onto it. "I have been thinking. If you can trust me to care for you and to do only what is best for your health, I can trust you with my past—some of it. If anything should happen—if your connection to me should be revealed—the knowledge might save your life, or at least buy you some time."

My heart fluttered with anticipation. "I have so many questions—"

"And you may or may not get the answers you want. All I ask is that you be quiet, and listen."

"I can do that."

"Are you sure?"

I grinned in response to the wry humor in his voice. "Here." I stretched out my hand. "I will hold your hand as you speak, and when I have a question, I will squeeze it. Then you can choose whether or not to pause your tale and allow the inquiry."

He inhaled, slow and deep, and then his broad palm and thick fingers engulfed my whole hand.

"Your hand is so small," he said in a wondering tone.

"But it is strong."

"It is. Like your spirit."

Palm to palm as we were, I could feel the thrum of his pulse and the heat of his skin, the soft scrape of the calluses on the heel of his hand and on the pads of his fingers. A sudden urge wakened in my heart—to lift that work-worn hand to my lips and soothe it with kisses.

My father complained frequently about the wanton, unpredictable emotions of women. Ever since I arrived at the Horseman's cabin, I seemed to be suffering from them more than ever—yearning for the Horseman one minute, running from him the next. Though perhaps my feelings would have been natural for any human in this confusing situation. After all, the Horseman himself seemed rather conflicted, buffeted by a storm of different emotions whenever he was around me. Usually those emotions ran the gamut from frustration and annoyance to sorrow or sarcastic amusement. In truth, most men I knew could be just as emotional as any woman—some even more so.

"Where to begin?" The Horseman's thumb rubbed a slow circle over the top of my hand. "You wonder why I would have to kill you, if you discovered my identity. It is because I operate under the will of someone else, someone who will protect their identity at all costs. As a dullahan, I am controlled by the magic circlet around my neck."

I squeezed his hand, and he sighed. "Already?"

"When did you receive the circlet? Were you born with it? Did it grow with you, or did you have to get a new one every year?"

"That is more than one question."

"Please?"

"A dullahan infant is born with the *gun cheann* spell etched into the skin of its throat, as the original curse dictated. Do not ask me about the source of the original curse—our race has many different tales to explain it, and none of them match each other. But each dullahan baby must have the *Colbh Droma* rite performed before its twelve-month, or it dies. During that rite, usually performed by a druid, the golden collar is formed. It is magical, so yes, its shape alters as the child grows.

"Dullahan walk the line between Death and Life. Their original purpose was to give humans power, a defense against the wicked attacks of Unseelie Fae. A human could speak a particular spell, perform a blood ritual, and become bound to a specific dullahan or an entire family of dullahan. Then the dullahan would be bound to serve the will of that human. Ideally, a human would use such power to defend their villages and families against terrors like shapeshifters, dark Fae, and the monsters of old. But of course, humans most often use a dullahan against their fellow man, to wreak vengeance or to claim power."

My grip tightened on his hand, but this time he did not stop speaking. "You are going to ask how the collar works. Once someone has bonded to a dullahan like me, they become the *Ceannaire*, the master of that dullahan. When the Ceannaire has a target in mind for death, all they need to do is speak the spell written on the collar, along with the name of the individual to be killed. The order can also be given in writing. The instant I read or hear an order from my Ceannaire, I must carry it out. The change is nearly instantaneous—my skull separates from my body and I must ride to kill. Until the murder is done and the victim's head is removed, I remain headless. Sometimes I meet my Ceannaire in the forest, and they give me a command, or they send a hawk with a strip of paper around its leg."

I interrupted without bothering to squeeze his hand. "Could you simply refuse to meet them, or refuse to open the missives?"

"I cannot. The band around my throat compels me to acknowledge the messages and to do the Ceannaire's will. The longer I am bound to their service, the more difficult it is for me to resist."

"How did it happen? How were you bound to such a person? Who is it?"

"A spell lies upon me that prevents me from saying the name—and even if there were no spell, I would not tell you. The knowledge would put you in too much danger. My Ceannaire would lose everything if sh—if they were discovered—"

I latched onto the half-word he dropped. "You almost said *she*."

"Damn it." He jerked his hand away.

"It's all right. I am not much closer to the discovery. So, if I understand correctly—you do not have a choice when it comes to the killing?"

"Yes. Dullahan can speak the spell themselves and perform murders of their own volition, to suit their own ends. But they may not work against the wellbeing of the Ceannaire or their bloodline. So I cannot free myself that way."

"Damn it." I echoed his curse, the words deliciously forbidden on my tongue. "That is what I was going to suggest."

"I would not willingly end any life," he said. "I am not a killer. Not by choice. It is a terrible sorrow, taking a life."

"You are a servant yourself." Realization dawned in my mind. "That is why you are determined to serve the medical needs of the laborers in this region. You know how helpless they feel, how they are poorly paid for their services, scarcely able to afford what they need." I fumbled for his hand, and he allowed me to recapture it. "When I come into my inheritance, I plan to pay our servants good wages. Far more than my father does."

His fingers pressed mine. "That is a bold statement, Katrina. Do you understand how that will impact on your father's holdings?"

"No," I replied truthfully. "I do not understand all of it, not yet. But I know that it is the right thing to do. I am not afraid of working hard with my own hands, or of paying laborers what they deserve. That is what I will do."

"And your partner in this endeavor—will it be one of these suitors you mentioned? Brom Van Brunt, perhaps?"

"No!"

The Horseman chuckled at my decisive answer. "I thought you said he was a friend."

"I am beginning to realize that many of my friends do not share my values of kindness and decency. Brom is cruel. And he is not without guilt for Ichabod's death. Although I suppose I bear a share of the guilt as well."

"You?" The Horseman scoffed. "I do not believe it."

"I was going to try to help Ichabod." My voice dropped to a shaky murmur. "Brom was beating him out of jealousy and spite—but when I approached them, Ichabod was flung against the sharp branch I held, and it pierced his throat. I—I killed him."

"An accident, pure and simple." The Horseman tightened his grip on my fingers. I did not even mind that his palm had become sweaty; the comforting strength of it was the only thing keeping me from bursting into sobs.

"An accident is merely a situation in which someone should have been more careful." I repeated my mother's favorite words. "It is an error that could have been avoided through prudence and diligence."

"That seems a harsh way to live," said the Horseman. "It leaves no room for human frailty, for mistakes."

"Mistakes—like the way I rode after Ichabod instead of leaving him to his own devices? If I had not ridden after him—"

"He would be dead anyway, at my hand," the Horseman intercepted.

"Where do you think he is now? Heaven?"

"Heaven is a difficult concept for someone like me." The chair creaked as he shifted his weight. "I am technically one of the Fae myself, and we have our own ideas about the world, and the gods, and dimensions beyond what can be seen. There is a theory among my people—" His words cut off abruptly, and tension sang through every muscle of his hand where it contacted mine. "Hush a moment."

I heard it then—the unmistakable rhythm of hoofbeats, and a faint whinny.

"Someone is here." He began swearing again. "Get up, quickly. You will have to hide under the bed, Katrina—I'm sorry for any pain this may cause you." He hauled me out of the bed and helped me scoot sideways under it, on my belly. "Hurry. Watch your head. A little further in, I can still see your foot. There now—stay. And for the love of all that is holy, be quiet!"

4

There was a brief scuffle as the Horseman stuffed a few telltale items under the bed with me and rearranged the blankets, letting them drape low over the side to conceal my hiding place. His footsteps vibrated through the wood floor as he went out into the hall. A door squeaked, and then I heard muttered greetings.

Lying blindfolded and wounded under the Horseman's bed was not something I had ever expected to do. I did not like it. A faint smell of rot and damp earth drifted up to my nose through a crack in the floorboards, and something leggy skittered over my hand. I bit my tongue to keep from yelping, and then my mouth tasted like copper and salt.

Two sets of feet were coming nearer—nearer—they entered the room, and I heard the second voice—a woman's voice. A familiar voice, one whose melody I had heard all my life. The sweet, clear tones of Anika Van Brunt.

"Usually you are a little more gracious when I have taken the trouble to travel all the way up here to your disgusting cabin," she said. "But this time I had to invite myself in. Your manners are failing, Eamon."

"I apologize," the Horseman muttered.

No. This could not be happening. Why would Anika Van Brunt be visiting the Horseman?

Unless—

No. Impossible.

"May I offer you some water? Bread?" The Horseman's voice sounded higher than usual, and inwardly I willed for him to be calm, to conceal his nerves and his fear from this woman—this woman I thought I knew—

"No, thank you," Anika replied. "Let us get straight to business. Clearly you disposed of the schoolmaster as I requested—well done. My neighbors are not sure whether he was a victim of the Horseman or simply took a new position in another town. There's already a rumor circulating that Ichabod found a wealthy widow to marry, somewhere beyond the valley. It was perfectly executed."

"I am glad you are pleased with the outcome."

"But I am *not* pleased. My triumph over the insipid schoolmaster has been tarnished by the mysterious disappearance of the Van Tassel girl. You know I didn't want her dead. I wanted Ichabod out of the way because he has been babbling about the dullahan for weeks, to this person and that—and also because he seemed to be stealing Katrina's affections away from my darling Brom. But now Katrina is nowhere to be found, and my son is telling everyone that the Horseman killed both her and Ichabod. Men have been searching the forests and ponds for her body. What happened, Eamon? She is the perfect bride for my son. If you have killed her, I shall be very displeased."

"I did not kill her," said the Horseman. "Though I did catch a glimpse of her that night. She ran off while I was slaying Ichabod. Perhaps she got lost. Perhaps someone else attacked her. Remember the pickpocket who came through a while back, the one you had me kill after he stole your favorite brooch? And those two ruffians I dispatched a month ago, the pair you suspected of being deserters, or pirates? You told me yourself that more unsavory characters are coming into the valley of late. The girl could have encountered someone of that sort."

"I suppose so. Or she could have gotten lost, as you say," mused Anika. "Though she knows the woods and fields well. She and Brom used to roam the glades together—we permitted it, you see, because they were to be married when they grew older. They should have been married by now! Curse her foolish mother for not pressing the girl into it when she was sixteen, or eighteen! The knot should have been tied back then. When they delayed again, last year, I nearly ordered Brom to take her anyway and get her with child, so the marriage would *have* to happen. And now she is lost, you say, or defiled and murdered by ruffians? You swear you did not harm her?"

"I swear to you, my mistress—I did not lay a violent hand on the girl."

"Oh, very well. I can see you speak the truth." Anika blew out a frustrated breath. "Where shall I find another such wife for my Brom? Katrina was perfect. Beautiful, well-shaped, intelligent, good-humored—with plenty of lands and wealth to keep me and my son comfortable for years. Such a fine position we would have had! So many little luxuries, and such well-appointed rooms in that big house—I have always loved it."

"You might have had to wait a long time to enjoy it," said the Horseman. "I saw Baltus Van Tassel recently—he is still a hale and hearty man."

"Oh, I was going to have you knock him off, a year or so after the wedding," said Anika carelessly. "It's so wonderfully convenient, having you at my disposal, dear Eamon. I know you disapprove of some of my methods, but it is a good life for you here, is it not? Quiet and peaceful, far from noise and trouble. And you have everything you need. I make sure of that, don't I?"

"Yes, my mistress."

"Well, I want you to ride tonight—not to kill, but to look for the wayward Katrina. Perhaps she is huddled in a distant copse, or has taken refuge in some old shack. My hope is fading, because it has been two days—but we must keep up our spirits! And if she is not to be found—well—I suppose I must alter the plan I have held dear for decades, and find another wife for my Brom. A pity that the Van Tassels have no other heirs!"

"They must be heartbroken," the Horseman said.

"Oh, Eamon my dear, don't I know it! The wails and whimpers I have had to endure from Ilse Van Tassel—the floods of tears she has shed into the shoulder of my good dress—you would not believe it. I do feel sorry for her, the poor thing. She may be a stiff-necked, silly woman, but I consider her a friend."

A chair shifted, and Anika's feet tapped the floor. "I should be going. I do not like to linger here. Remember, our connection must be kept strictly secret. You are limiting your visits to town, yes? Only once a month for necessities, wearing your scarf and hat, speaking to no one?"

"Yes, my mistress."

Anika released a musical ripple of laughter. "You do know how to appease me, Eamon. Calling me 'mistress'—such a delight. Come, give me a kiss."

Silence followed, while I ground my teeth into my knuckle.

"Come now." Anika's voice shifted into a new key, cold and slippery as an eel in dark water. "Because of your reluctance to obey, it shall be a pair of kisses. Be grateful that I am a godly woman and I value my virtue—otherwise I might require more of you, Eamon my darling."

A soft rustle of movement followed, and then a slight smacking repeated once, and again. A low hum of satisfaction passed from Anika. Acid seeped into the back of my throat and I bit my knuckle harder.

Footsteps exited the room, and then hoofbeats drummed away.

I stayed under the bed until the Horseman's heavy footfalls returned and halted near me.

"Katrina," he said.

Tears clouded my eyes and bile threatened to lurch from my stomach. My fingers, my arms, my whole body was shaking.

"She is gone, Katrina. I—I am so sorry. Will you come out?"

"No." My voice was a broken squeak.

"I suppose I can tell you everything now."

"I don't know if I can bear it."

"She was not always this hard of heart. Or maybe she was, and she fooled me, as she fooled you and your family." With a slow thump and a scrape of boots, the Horseman sits down on the floor beside the bed. His words are sluggish, as if every sentence is being hauled unwilling from his mouth. "The first person she had me kill was her husband, Cor Van Brunt. He beat her, you see, and he took her body roughly every night, without compassion or affection. She was justified in wanting him dead. He had begun to beat young Brom, too, and she would not stand for it. She needed a way to destroy him without being hung for his murder. And she had heard whispers about my bloodline, and the things we could do. It was only a matter of time before she discovered the truth."

"How did she hear whispers of your bloodline?"

"Her husband was married once before, to my father's sister. My aunt died in childbirth, along with her baby, Cor Van Brunt's firstborn. My father suspected that she confided the truth of her Fae nature to Cor, and he killed her and the baby out of sheer terror, but we could never prove it. And my mother insisted that we keep up appearances and retain the family connection for years after my aunt's death. It's likely Anika heard some hint about my family through Cor, perhaps when he was drunk and feeling confessional. Or perhaps she caught a rumor elsewhere. After all, my people lived quietly in this hollow long before the Dutch arrived to settle it."

"And your parents? Where are they now?"

"Being dullahan does not protect you from the plague. We heal a little better than humans, but we can sicken and die. In my parents' case it was smallpox. My father died first. My mother held out long enough to help me and my brother Rory pull through it, but then she collapsed, insensible with fever. She never woke again. I was ten, and Rory was twelve—we did not know what to do, or how to help her. We buried my parents together, not far from this cottage."

Sympathy cut through my heart, a knife-blade spreading the echo of his pain. Biting my lip, I scooted out from beneath the bed, moving slowly so as not to wrench my wound. The Horseman—Eamon—laid a hand on my head so I would not bump it against the bedframe as I slid free. When I was clear of the bed, I sat up stiffly and felt for his shoulder, rubbing it with my fingers. "I am so sorry."

"It is the reality of mortal life," he said dolefully. "Afterward, Rory and I went to live in a distant town with a family friend. We were free of any master at the time, and no one knew the myth of the dullahan in that busy place. We covered our golden bands with cravats or scarves. I became an apothecary's apprentice, and later a surgeon's assistant. My brother worked in a factory for a time, then finally decided to go West."

"That's when you came back here. To provide medical care for the servants."

"Yes. I was nineteen, and full of righteous enthusiasm. And I suppose I felt a connection to this valley—something unfinished. But before I could begin my good work, Anika approached me with her sad tale of nightly rapes and daily beatings. I wanted to help her, and I knew that without a master, I was vulnerable—anyone could take control of me and use me as an assassin. So I let myself be bound to her, for our mutual benefit. 'Only one task,' she told me, 'and then you can do as you like.' But one task became two, and three, and more. She ordered me to spend my days up here, hidden away, except for the occasional trip to the market. But she did not say what I must do with my nights—so whenever I can, I visit the servants throughout the valley and do what I can to help those who are sick or suffering."

I gasped, pulling away from him. "You are the Night Angel!"

"The *what*?"

"One of my father's servants told me of the Night Angel who visits their sick. I wasn't sure who it could be—but now I know. It's you."

"I—I did not know they gave me that name. It does not suit me at all."

"So you prefer your real name—Eamon."

An exasperated breath burst from him. "And there it is—all my secrets have been bared to you. Are you satisfied?"

"Not quite." And before he could stop me, I pushed the blindfold upward, off my head, and I tossed it aside.

When I opened my eyes, the first thing I saw was his face. Sparkling dark eyes, surprisingly soft, like a night sky flecked with stars. Heavy brows pulled together in rebuke, and short dark hair stuck up in unruly spikes above a broad forehead. He had a thin, straight nose, and skin tanned from hard labor under the sun. His mouth, shaped just like Cupid's own bow, skewed up at one side, because despite his frowning eyebrows he was half-smiling at me.

Something about that half-smile twitched in my brain, triggering a hazy memory. "Did I meet you once before? When I was young—yes! A Christmas party at the Van Brunts' place—"

That night I had been introduced to several of their distant relatives, including a tall, dark-haired boy who refused to play hide-and-seek with me and Brom and the other children. The boy had kept his collar turned up as he hunched against the wall in a corner.

"Every time we chose a new game, I came over and asked you to play," I said slowly.

Eamon's eyes widened. "The little golden girl. You kept popping up, trying to draw me into your games. And finally you brought me a book of short poems—"

"—and I asked you to read to me. And you gave me a half-smile—"

"—and I said yes."

"You read to me until I grew sleepy, and it was time to go home. Brom and I were maybe five, so you would have been nine—" I stopped, realization dawning. I had met him the year before his parents died.

"This is strange, isn't it?" I said. "Knowing that we met before, when we were so young?"

"Very. But it warms my heart as well. You were the only person at that party who made me feel seen, and wanted. It's a feeling that has been all too rare since then."

His dark eyes shone and his mouth inched higher at one corner. The urge to wrap him in my arms and cover him with kisses slammed through my body like a rockslide, primal and nearly irresistible. I could scarcely hold myself back, and instead tried to be content with devouring him with my eyes, from his crisp jawline, to his sinewy neck sealed with the gold band, down to his hulking shoulders. His shirt hung open, forming a V through which I glimpsed a scattering of dark hair on his chest. Every bit of him was huge and brutally male; but I knew the gentleness of those thick fingers, and the compassion in the heart beating under all that packed muscle.

Even if I had daydreamed for a hundred hours, I could not have imagined such a perfect match, so suited to me physically and mentally and philosophically. Except for the tiny, miniscule, infinitesimal problem of his Fae nature—his life as a dullahan, an enslaved killer.

Mine, whispered my traitorous soul. *He will be mine alone, and no other woman's.*

"You are staring at me." His smile faded. "Do I frighten you?"

"Not at all." I reached for his face, petting the stubbled skin of his jaw. He tensed, but he did not pull away; in fact, his breathing sped up a fraction. A familiar impulse seized me—the urge to play with him, to see how far I could push him—except this time, I truly wanted to go wherever the game might take us. This time, no one was there to chaperone, or to restrain me.

This time, no one had to know.

The only thing holding me back was this confounded wound in my back. Damn that ill-fated branch.

"What about me?" My fingers wandered along his neck, over the gold band, my nails teasing the symbols on it. "Do I frighten you?"

My hand slid lower, skimming his collarbone, and my thumb traced the dip of his throat.

He caught my wrist, his eyes hardening. "You want me to say 'yes,' don't you?" The grip on my wrist tightened. "You want me to say that you frighten me, that you have power over me."

"Maybe..." I frowned, trying to pull away.

"I don't have the stomach for your games, Katrina. I—wait—what is this, here?" He nodded to the scarlet bite marks on my knuckle.

"I bite my hand sometimes, if I'm in pain, or too full of nerves or anger. It helps me regain control. I had to do it several times while Anika was here."

"But you're hurting yourself."

"Sometimes I don't have a choice—I have to find an outlet, or go mad." My face heated under his inspection, and I tried to halt the flow of words—but I had never spoken of this habit to a living soul, and suddenly I could not stop myself. "I started it in school, when I had to sit still for hours. And I do it even now, when I'm in service, or at tea, or in a sewing circle—and there's nowhere to go, no way to escape, and my legs feel restless, like they will start dancing around the room all on their own—or if I am so full of agitated thoughts that I want to scream. Then I bite myself, rather than screaming, or dancing, or running away. It helps."

In his eyes I saw no judgment, only sympathy. "You really don't like to rest and be still, do you?"

"I need to move, and do things. That has always been my way."

"And I have been asking you to be idle, and to do nothing." He grimaced. "I am sorry. I will read to you tonight, if you like. I am tired, but I have enough left in me for a few chapters, I think. Will that amuse you?" His grin blazed into my very soul, a burst of dazzling sunshine. "Just like old times."

"Old *time*," I corrected, a little breathless from the glory of that smile. "You read to me *once*."

His lips parted as if he would answer, but he simply kept staring into my eyes. "Your eyes are such a dark blue. Like—like blueberries."

I smirked. "You are not used to delivering compliments to women, I take it."

"No, I am not." A blush colored his cheeks, and he lunged to his feet, clearing his throat. "So. Dinner. And then—a book. Yes. You get back in bed."

But his gruffness held no threat for me anymore. Truthfully my wound was aching, and I wanted to lie down; but not as much as I wanted his touch. "And if I refuse to get into bed?"

"Then I will have to put you there."

I crossed my arms over my chest and smiled up at him. From my vantage point, sitting on the floor beside the bed, his frame towered gigantic above me, so immense that my breath stopped for a second. I remembered how fearsome he looked astride his horse, dressed in that big coat. A flicker of desire teased along the sliver of space between my thighs.

He reached for me, and a thrill shot through my stomach.

Big warm hands closed around my arms, drawing me gently upward until I stood nearly against his body. The air between us sparked with energy, coiling and tightening. I could not breathe properly.

I looked up into the Horseman's face and smirked, the practiced simper of a true coquette. *You will kiss me*, I ordered him mentally, pursing my lips slightly. I knew how pink and luscious they were. He would not be able to resist.

But instead of lust, anger flashed through his eyes. He backed me onto the bed, swinging my legs and body into place on the mattress in one swift motion. I barely had the chance to savor the touch of his hands on my thigh and shoulder before it was over, and he moved away.

"You can stop the act, Katrina," he threw over his shoulder. "I am not one of your suitors."

He disappeared into the hall, where I could hear him fumbling around with the shelves and their contents, swearing intermittently.

Confused, I did a mental checklist of my charms. All my best qualities were still present—but it had been a while since I last bathed. My hair was greasier than usual, lying flat against my head instead of sweeping in loose golden waves. And my body—I sniffed my armpit and winced, both at the pain in my back and at the smell of my skin. The Horseman should not be so choosy, especially when he was rarely as fresh as a daisy himself. However, if my dirtiness offended him, I could remedy that, with his help. And a new plan for his seduction unfolded in my mind—fantasies I had indulged in all too often during Sunday service, or at night in my room, scenes I never thought would be possible in real life.

    He stalked back into the room and set about peeling and chopping potatoes. Their earthy smell, and the thunk of the knife, and the popping hiss of the fire filled the space between us. Lying on my side, I watched the Horseman's hands, flexing and shifting so easily over the knife as he cut slices of potato. Such magnificent hands.

    "Stop staring at me, Katrina," he said.

    "I will not."

    He growled something under his breath.

    "What was that?"

    "I said, I should never have told you all those things about myself, and my life. I thought you would be more cautious of me, once you knew the truth. But you seem more fascinated than ever." He shook his head. "Do you have a death wish?"

    "No. But I have several life wishes. Do you want to hear them?"

"I do not. Ow!" He inspected his finger, which oozed glittering red blood. "You see what you've done?" He reached for a cloth and snapped it out before wrapping it around the injury. "You distracted me."

"Did I?" I lifted my eyebrows and hunched my right shoulder, causing the loose tunic to slip down. The top half of my right breast emerged above the edge. "I was thinking I should bathe later. I'm beginning to smell like you. What do you think, Eamon? Will you help me bathe?"

He stared, dumfounded. "I do not know what to do with you."

"Feed me. Bathe me. Read to me. I am not that complicated, Eamon."

"Stop saying my name."

"No." I grinned at him.

He growled in frustration and began tossing potato chunks into the pot over the fire. "Why didn't I leave you on the bridge?"

"You said that before. Do you really wish you had left me to die?"

"Yes."

His words doused me like a bucketful of icy water. All my playful confidence drained away.

Perhaps I wasn't nearly as charming or beautiful as I thought. Perhaps I was merely annoying, and smelly, and troublesome. Here, in the hills, in this cabin, I existed as an injured burden, not a glittering heiress to lands and goods envied by everyone in the valley.

Take away all the livestock and orchards, the luxurious clothes and perfumes, the fine coiffures and social standing—and what was I, really? Books and long rambles in the forest, fishing and whittling, a motley collection of wicked desires and moral ideals that would make my neighbors gasp or jeer by turns. A mess of dreams and longings, stitched together with a spirit far more fragile than I realized.

Stiffly, painfully, I turned my body over in the bed until my back was facing the Horseman. And I let the tears flow, hot and silent, over my face and into the pillow.

Eamon woke me with a warm hand on my shoulder. "The food is ready."

"I don't want any." But even as I spoke, my stomach rumbled audibly.

"I think your body says otherwise. And as your physician, I must insist that you eat."

"Very well." I hauled myself to a sitting position, flinching at the stab of pain. "But I don't promise to like it."

He gave me one of his half-smiles and handed over a bowl of stew. While I ate, he paced doggedly in and out of the room, carrying water, heating it, filling the tub he used the other day. The sight of the tub triggered a vivid memory of his body, the muscles highlighted in amber firelight.

When I finished eating, he collected my bowl and pointed to a chair beside the tub. "I have laid out soap and cloths for washing and drying. There's a bucket for rinsing as well. You should be careful not to get your wound too wet."

"How am I supposed to wash my hair and everything else while keeping the wound dry? That's impossible." I hissed the last word through clenched teeth. I had planned to lure him into helping me bathe, and then—some kind of seduction? Now I could not imagine trying to seduce him, when I knew it would only lead to further humiliation and rejection. But the fact remained, that I could not bathe properly *and* keep my wound dry without his help.

"There are some things you cannot ask a man to do," the Horseman said tightly.

"Did I ask?" I snapped.

"No, but—"

"Leave. I will manage somehow." I pushed myself from the bed and stood up, shaky, willing the stars to stop dancing across my eyes. "You have made it clear that I am too much trouble. So I will impose on your hospitality only this night, and tomorrow I will walk home. At least in the valley there are people who do not wish me dead. Now leave, unless you are prepared to face the extraordinarily distasteful sight of my body."

Fire gleamed in his eyes—but whether it was anger or something else, I could not tell. "I have emptied your bedpans, Katrina. I think I can handle distasteful."

I poured the full force of my anger through my eyes. "Are you...comparing...my body...to *shit*?"

"No!" he exclaimed. "I'm only saying—"

"What *are* you saying? Because after baring your soul to me, you seem suddenly eager to insult me in every way you can think of. Is that any way to treat someone who knows your secret?"

"No—I—are you trying to blackmail me into being kind to you?"

"I prefer kindness to death wishes, yes."

"I don't wish you dead!" His voice rose in volume and force, and I fisted my hands to brace myself against it. "I only said that because, after telling you all those things about myself, I feel—exposed. Weak. You make me feel helpless, undone, and vulnerable in a way that I cannot—that I do not—I hate feeling this way, and it makes me cruel."

Understanding latched into place inside me, like a peg slipping neatly into a hole, like a drawer skimming smoothly shut.

"You are not cruel," I said. "You have little authority over your life, so you control what you can—your secret. And when that is revealed, you become anxious, and afraid. I understand. These 'games,' as you call them—the way I play with men—it is my own way of taking control, of making the choice and the process more about me and what I want. But it has never really worked. I am left always unsatisfied, always knowing that my options for love are limited, that my path in life is already marked out, that marriage will be a prison of propriety. Why do you think I have put it off as long as I can? So yes, Eamon—I understand why you are struggling. You gave up a bit of control, and it unsettled you." I stepped nearer, laying a hand on his arm. "But you are neither a bargaining chip nor a game to me. I owe you my life, in the most literal sense. You have shown me kindness and consideration—you speak to me as an equal, which even my suitors rarely do. You have opened your deepest truth to me. Your compassion, your humor, your intelligence—and yes, your beauty—they affect me deeply. But I understand if you have no inclination toward me. I suppose I am not very appealing, after all."

The Horseman's hands landed on either side of my head, and for the barest second, I thought perhaps I had gone too far, and that he was going to wrench my skull clean off my spine. But instead he planted his lips on mine, and a lightning-sharp thrill ripped through my body.

He tasted like the stew, warm and savory and salty, with a tantalizing spiciness that was uniquely him—his taste, like his scent, roughly male, with an edge of something wild and Otherworldly—a crackling whisper of magic. I lifted my arms, curling them around his neck. Kissing was better than coy glances, better than sugared cakes, better than wine, better than books—his *mouth*—my *god*. And his tongue—the Devil himself did not have such a tongue, capable of eliciting a manic tingle between my thighs as he swept it along my teeth and across the arch of my mouth. I whimpered and pressed closer to him, heedless of the pain spiking in my wound.

But Eamon pulled back, as if he could sense my pain somehow. His palm drifted down my back to the bandage. "I am sorry. I let myself be carried away."

"You should be carried away more often," I whispered. "So—you do think I am appealing."

He let out a shuddering sigh. "Katrina."

"What? I think you should be able to say it. You think I am beautiful."

"You know you are beautiful. But that is only one of many things I find compelling about you."

"Tell me."

He swallowed, his throat shifting beneath the band. "Your bathwater is getting cold."

"Then—help me bathe first."

His chest swelled against mine with his intake of breath. "Are you sure?"

"Yes."

I stepped away, carefully inching the tunic over my head without stretching my back too much. I let the shirt fall at my feet, and I stood bare before him. I had always longed to reveal myself to a man, to be completely naked before admiring eyes, to share the beauty of my form, that no one else ever got to see.

And this was my chance.

Eamon said, "Oh god." He turned away and gripped the back of the chair he'd placed beside the tub.

"As a physician, you should be accustomed to human bodies," I said primly, using his rigid arm to steady myself as I stepped into the tub.

"This is different, and you know it." He looked at me, his cheekbones painted scarlet with embarrassment, his eyes glimmering with desire he was clearly struggling to repress.

"Am I the first woman you've seen naked?"

"Other than cadavers—yes. Patients only reveal the parts that require my attention, and it is a different scenario entirely—it doesn't affect me—not like this."

A grin teased my mouth, but I resisted it, for his sake. He did not need me gloating over his embarrassment. He was like an injured dog, all sorrow and soft brown eyes, but willing to bite if he sensed a threat. I had to be careful with him, to gently coax him out of his isolation. Honesty, it seemed, was the way to his heart. I must earn his entire trust, as he now had mine.

To distract him from his embarrassment, I said, "What will happen to my injury if it gets wet?"

"Um...the wound could soften and reopen. Too much moisture can make a wound inflamed and cause it to ooze. I have a theory that air and water can carry harmful particles into incisions or punctures, and as those particles grow, they disturb the natural healing process. The body becomes feverish and inflamed while trying to push out the invading entities."

While he spoke, I picked up the soap and began to wash myself. It was a plain lye variety with no infused lavender or rose petals like my soaps at home; but it would do the job well enough.

"Wash my back, would you?" I handed the soap to Eamon. He cleared his throat and stepped around the tub, sliding the bar across my shoulder blades. Then a wet glide down my spine, with a detour to avoid the wound. A slow, slippery circle across one cheek of my rear. And then the other.

Every nerve ending of my body, every sense I owned, wakened, rapt and exquisitely sensitive. Barely breathing, I stood still, helpless to the slick desire gathering inside me. The small room cradled the warmth of the fire, and the lingering aroma of savory stew mingled with the fragrance of wood smoke. The hot water soothed my aching feet and legs so beautifully that I wanted to immerse myself wholly in it. A big, beautiful man stood behind me, smelling of earth and horse and fresh autumn wind, bathing my body with tender care. No sound but the drip and slosh of the water, and the squelch of the soap in Eamon's hand, and the crack and hiss of the flames in the fireplace.

After skimming the backs of my thighs with the soap, Eamon collected my limp hand and tucked the bar into it. "I think you can do the other bits yourself."

He scooped water into his palm and carefully rinsed the soapy paths he had traced across my skin.

When he was done, I tossed my hair forward, letting it hang in front of my face. Eamon helped me lather and rinse it while he spoke of wounds, and pustules, and sepsis, and rot. Then he told me of a burn victim who had been treated by the surgeon to whom he was apprenticed. He explained, in horrific detail, how they used maggots to gently clean the dead flesh away so the healthy tissues could recover.

My desire definitely waned during his lecture. Perhaps that was his intention—though whether he was doing it for my benefit or for his was another question.

Finally I straightened, twisting water from my hair. "Do you speak like this to other civilized women?"

"I did, once." He winced. "I tried courting a young woman when I was eighteen. It did not go well."

"Fortunately for you, I do not mind indelicate speech. In fact I could do with more of it—only not about wounds this time, I beg you."

He hesitated, looking down at his hands. "There is not much more to tell, anyway. My master finally told me I would never be a good surgeon. I do not have the slender fingers for it, you see."

"Nonsense. You have done much good with those hands," I told him. "And I'll wager you could put them to all kinds of delightful uses."

His gaze snapped to mine, and I saw the heat of my own desire reflected in his dark eyes.

"Help me out of the tub," I whispered.

He gave me his hand, and I stepped out, nearly into his arms.

"I am feeling a little weak and dizzy," I said. "Will you dry me off?"

Eamon grabbed a dry cloth and passed it over my shoulders, my collarbones. He pressed it lightly against my breasts, until I thought I would go mad from the teasing contact.

"Are you trying to drive me insane?" I hissed.

He hesitated, his brows contracting. "Not at all. I am trying to be respectful."

"Well, stop it. I give you leave to be as damn disrespectful as you like."

"What does that mean?" A note of painful confusion entered his voice.

I drew in a deep breath. He was about to bolt again, so I had to be careful, and considerate, and very, very clear about my intentions.

"It means that you do not have to fight with yourself anymore." I tilted my head, giving him a soft smile, my lashes hooding my eyes. "Breathe. Feel the desire, and let yourself take what you want. You have my enthusiastic permission."

He glared at me for a moment, then tossed the cloth right over my head, blocking my vision. "I will not take you here in my home, while you are wounded."

I struggled to get the fabric off my face. "You could be very careful with me. No one would ever know." The cloth fell into the tub, but I did not care. I moved closer to him, my breasts grazing his shirt.

"What if you became with child? What then? You are so damned impulsive. Do you ever think about the results of your actions, Katrina?" He ran both hands over his head, his features contorted with frustration.

Truthfully, I had not thought of pregnancy. Embarrassed, I lashed him with the first words that came to mind. "You are right—I am impulsive. We cannot all be cautious, cold-hearted eunuchs like you. Are you sure your head is the only thing that comes off when you change?"

"A eunuch, am I?" He placed one hand on my lower back and hauled my hips against his. I could feel him, hard and eager despite his protests.

Delighted, I looked up. "If you are concerned about getting me with child, there are things we can do that are—not exactly *that*." I gave him the same winsome smile I used long ago, when we were children at a party—except now, there was a good deal more of the devil in it. "We can always read tomorrow. Do you want to play with me?"

5

I lay on my side in the Horseman's bed, entirely naked, my skin warm and alive. I faced the wall instead of the room this time, and between me and the wall lay the Horseman himself, shirtless at my insistence, his handsome face flushed scarlet at the idea of what we were about to do.

"We will begin," I said, "with more kissing. And then—allow yourself to do what feels natural. Your hands may wander at your pleasure, as mine will."

He cleared his throat. "But how will I know what to do, for you?" Though he spoke gruffly, there was a plaintive note that delighted my soul.

"I will guide you. I have pleased myself before, many times."

His downcast eyes flicked up to mine for an instant, and he ran his tongue over his lip in a manner I found most distracting.

"Do you think me very wicked?" I whispered.

"Yes," he breathed. "And no. You are clearly a person with higher morals than many in these times—true moral goodness, respect for all your fellow humans, not just those who look like you. Even to me, a monster, you have shown such compassion—" He hesitates, his fingers playing with an unraveled bit of the blanket between us. "Your beauty alone does not compel me to want you—it's your irreverent, buoyant spirit—your sweet fire—your conversation, both amusing and intelligent. Even when I am piqued at you, I cannot really be angry. You know who I am, what I have done, and still you smile at me—you *smile*, Katrina. How? How can you accept this—" he touched the band at his throat— "so readily?"

"It is a difference, like any other that may exist between people," I told him. "It is nothing you can control. You do not kill for the pleasure of it, and I believe harming others cleaves such agony into your soul that you can scarcely stand it, that you can hardly believe yourself worthy of communing with other people. That is the real reason you hide up here. Not only because your Ceannaire commands it, but because you do not think you deserve friendship, or companionship."

Tears glittered in his dark eyes, and he turned his head away. "How do you do that?" he asked. "You flay me open, reading my heart better than I can."

My own eyes prickled, the forewarning of coming tears. This was not what I had planned. I wanted amusement and mutual entertainment, not a confession, not an earnest baring of souls. But perhaps the revelation of ourselves would deepen the moment, and make the intimacy even more precious.

"I understand you, somehow," I whispered. "I think there are different languages of the heart, mystical and inaudible. And maybe we share a common language between us, you and I. Now, stop thinking so much, and kiss me."

He shifted nearer, until the tip of his nose brushed mine and his beautiful dark eyes filled my sight. When I looked into those eyes, I felt as if I stood on the brink of a hidden valley, all shadowed hollows and sunny hills and secret spaces no one else had visited. I alone was permitted to enter.

I nudged my face closer to his, until our lips nearly touched. My breath trickled into his parted mouth, and his sigh whispered over my tongue, and the sliver of space between our trembling lips pulsed with the delicious agony of desire.

I flicked my tongue out, sweeping his lower lip—tasting it, savoring its sensual curve. He tilted his face a fraction, and his lips grazed mine, softly, surely, pushing deeper. The tips of our tongues slipped over each other as we kissed, and kissed, and kissed again. Each fresh melding of our mouths was an epiphany, a flood of new sensations both glorious and torturous.

Eamon's broad hand cupped my cheek, his thumb caressing my skin. For what seemed like hours, he touched no other part of me. Knowing my own impatience, it was probably mere minutes, but my enflamed body craved more touches, more tenderness. When he finally slid his palm along my neck to my shoulder, I sighed with satisfaction, because it was about to begin, at last—what I had wanted for all these long years.

His hand stopped at my shoulder and stayed there.

I squirmed unhappily, then yelped as a flash of pain reminded me of my wound. The bandage around my belly was my only scrap of covering, and I chafed at its presence.

"Am I hurting you?" Eamon asked, removing his hand.

"No. But you are enraging me, because I want your touch everywhere."

"Beyond my medical duties, I have never been allowed to touch more than a woman's covered arm, or her hand," Eamon said. "You will forgive me if I am slow to do more. Seeing you, like this—it is overwhelming." His gaze traveled to my breasts, and he reached for one of them like a man enchanted, tracing the tip with his finger. He followed the curve of it, cupped its weight in his palm.

My eyes closed reflexively. "Yes. More of that."

For a while we did not speak. Our hands carried our meaning to each other—palms sweeping over skin, fingertips grazing sensitive places to elicit sweet sighs. When I had thoroughly explored every dip and groove of Eamon's chest and stomach, I slid a finger beneath the band of his trousers and arched an eyebrow at him. He removed the rest of his clothing immediately and returned to the bed, his face flaming again. I laid my hand flat against his scarlet cheek and kissed him tenderly until he relaxed.

And then, looking into his face, I touched the part of him that burned for me. Immense and well-shaped, it was altogether fascinating, the way it reacted to my tentative fingers. Eamon inhaled quick and sharp, his startled eyes staring into mine, and I gave him my most wicked smile.

All I had learned, I knew from whispers and half-heard conversations, and a few peeks into rooms or dark spaces where I was not supposed to be. For a proper Dutch girl, I had gathered a surprising amount of knowledge, and what I did not know I learned quickly from my Horseman's responses.

I pressed my lips to his throat right beneath the golden collar, kissed the line of his jaw, and then his mouth again, while I quickened the movement of my hand. He came undone in moments—his groans vibrated against my lips, and he gripped my shoulders to brace himself. His eyes were glazed, his hair sweat-damp, and his mouth so rosy I had to kiss it half a dozen more times.

"You beautiful monster," I whispered.

And he was beautiful—the curved muscle and flat planes of his stomach shining with a light sweat, his scent rich and tantalizing. I traced the edge of one massive collarbone, all the way to the hulking swell of his shoulder.

His chest slowed its heaving, and he rotated his body toward me. "Now it is your turn. Tell me what I should do."

First I adjusted my hips and arched one leg, and then I begged him to kiss me again—or at least I opened my mouth to beg and he immediately darted in to cover my lips with his own.

When he put his huge, warm hand between my legs, and one of those thick fingers dipped a little deeper than the others, I thought I might die from the sheer joy of wish fulfillment. He was clumsy, tentative, but I took his fingers in mine and showed him what to do.

"Like that. Oh," I sighed as he continued the rhythm I set.

He asked many questions, in a tone soft and innocent, but so filthy in its subject matter that I could hardly reply because each inquiry was a fresh wave of stimulation. Soon I was panting, trying hard not to arch my back or angle my hips, desperate for release but unable to move the way I needed to without suffering pain from my wound.

I gripped the Horseman's face. "Swear," I hissed. "Tell me the foulest words you know, in your deepest tones."

His right hand continued its good work, while he leaned forward and growled curses into my ear until I reached the peak I had been trying to scale and fell beyond it, into a shimmering haze of golden cloud and pink sunlight. He wrapped both arms around me and held me as I shuddered and gasped his name.

Then he pulled the blanket over both of us, and we lay, blissfully entangled, until sleep came.

I woke a few times in the night, prey to sickening dreams of blood and fire and dark forests. When I first arrived at the cabin, I had been too exhausted for such dreams to come, but now they plagued me whenever I closed my eyes. It was the greatest comfort to burrow between Eamon's powerful arms and know that the headless nightmare who haunted the firesides of Sleepy Hollow held no terror for me.

Eamon left the bed when first light gleamed through the chinks of the shuttered window. I luxuriated in the spot his body had heated, watching him bathe his chest and arms, shave his jaw, and clean his teeth with a bit of cloth and a sprig of mint. He brought me a mint leaf too, and I chewed it gratefully.

"You should move around a bit more today—carefully, of course," said Eamon. "A little walking would do you good. And I have something—someone—to show you."

"Someone?" I spoke through a mouthful of biscuit, quirking an eyebrow at him.

"Yes. A friend."

"I thought you didn't have friends."

"Not the human kind."

"Oh!" Understanding dawned, and I nearly dropped the blanket I had wrapped around my body. "It's your horse, isn't it? The big black creature that you ride when you're headless? It's real? I had imagined it emerging from Hell to serve you when you called for it."

Eamon shook his head. "No, Katrina, dullahan do not call up hellish steeds from the Otherworld. My horse is very real—he eats and sleeps and shits like any other."

"I am done with my breakfast." I set the rest of the biscuit down and pushed my plate away. "Let's go and see him."

"Not yet." Eamon pointed to the plate. "At least eat the sausage, and the slice of cheese. You need strength. You have lost too much weight already, since your accident."

"You sound like my mother," I grumbled. " 'Eat more pastries, Katrina. Have another bit of chicken, Katrina. Try this tart, Katrina. Men like a nice round woman with curves.' "

"Hm." He gave me one of his charming half-smiles. "I would like you in any form, whether you were the most waifish wisp or the plumpest, rosy-cheeked matron."

The bite of sausage nearly fell from my mouth. "That is one of the sweetest things anyone has ever said to me. How did you manage it without hurting yourself?"

He threw a dishcloth at me, and I jerked backwards to avoid it, without thinking. "Ow!"

"Your back?"

I nodded. "Just a pinch of pain. Not bad."

"Maybe we should put off our walk for another day—"

"No! I'm fine. I am eating, see?" I crammed the food into my mouth. "I am ready to go."

"What was that? I couldn't hear you around all the cheese and sausage—"

I balled up the dishcloth and hurled it back at him. Eamon caught it easily. He had made me breakfast in all his glowing shirtless glory and I nearly choked at the wondrous flex of his muscles when he caught my missile.

"Good Lord in Heaven," I said, when I could breathe once more. "Are you trying to kill me?"

"Swearing again." He clucked his tongue. "You need to wear something when we go out. You cannot run about naked in the forest like some woodland nymph."

Slowly I rose from my seat on the bed, lifting my chin haughtily despite my blanket-clad state. "I am afraid, good sir, that the best I can manage at present is an unsteady toddle. There will be no nymph-like running today."

"I will help you to dress, then. Not in the tunic you were wearing, though—it smells rather rank."

"A shame you sliced my dress open," I said. "That was a favorite gown of mine."

"I had to act quickly to save your life," Eamon retorted. "And the blood would never have come out, anyway."

"True. But what shall I wear?"

"I have some extra clothes in a trunk—some old things of mine from when I was younger. If the moths have not gotten to them, we may find something there."

He fetched the trunk and rooted through it. The clothes were surprisingly dry and whole, though they smelled a bit musty. Eamon shook out a pair of dark trousers with a drawstring waist, and then a loose white shirt with laces at the neck. "These will do."

He surveyed me at first like a tailor judging the size of a client—but when I let the blanket fall, his gaze intensified, devouring every inch of me. Just being watched by him was enough to turn my legs weak. My skin tightened, thrilling, as he stalked nearer. But when he reached me, he only kissed my forehead and then knelt, holding out the trousers for me to step into. He pulled the pants up, tightening them at my waist and then rolling the cuffs to a manageable length. His fingers lingered over the fine bones of my feet and ankles, tracing them with a kind of delicate wonder. Hiding a smile, I pulled on the shirt and settled it over my shoulders. It fell well past my waist, and hung open wide in the front. I left it unlaced, for the express purpose of teasing the Horseman with the partial view of my breasts.

Eamon held out the shoes I had worn that night on the bridge, and I slid my feet into them. My heart ached, remembering how I danced with Ichabod in these very shoes. How lightly he stepped, how intensely focused he was. How proudly he smiled when the dance ended.

At least he had that one night of joy—before I dashed his hopes. Before he—

"You look sad," said the Horseman. His brows drew together as he examined my face. "Does the clothing not suit? I think you look lovely in it."

"The clothes are fine." I smiled for him. "I am ready."

He paced behind me down the hall before sidling ahead to swing open the door. Clear sunlight, the kind that only comes on a crisp autumn day, washed into the hallway and over me. I put up my hand to shield my eyes as I edged into its faint warmth.

"It is chillier than I thought," said Eamon. "I will fetch you a blanket." He dodged back inside, while I moved out of the cabin.

Even from the inside, I had thought the cabin an oddly shaped structure, with its long hallway, like a stretched-out pantry, and the one big room. Eamon had apparently fetched the trunk of clothes from a back room, possibly a bedroom at one time, now used for storage. Now that I stood outside, I could see that the cabin's exterior was rough, but well-maintained—the logs were dry and solid, the chinking had been carefully mended to protect the interior from winter's cold. The roof appeared to be in good repair, with deep eaves to prevent rain from puddling right against the walls.

The cabin sat atop a grassy knoll, in a clearing bordered by flamboyant scarlet maples, aspens with their fluttering orange leaves, and oaks with foliage of rich amber or blood-red. Here and there, a hornbeam or beech tree shimmered golden-bronze or bright yellow. And the sky arched over it all, a joyful sweep of sun-bright blue and creamy clouds, like fluffy blobs of frosting. The scent of the world this morning was freshness incarnate, with the sweet tang of coming frost tickling my nostrils. The breeze teased the billowy sleeves of my borrowed shirt and tossed my hair around my shoulders.

I wanted to scream from sheer exuberance. I wanted to embrace the entire scene, absorb it into myself so I could carry the beauty of it with me always.

A blanket draped across my shoulders, and I drew it close, looking up at the Horseman. Until now, I had only seen him by firelight. The sun turned his tan to rich bronze, and the wind ruffled up his already unruly hair so that it stuck out in spikes all over his head, like an inky, thorny halo. He wore a shirt now, loose like mine. A slow smile creased his cheeks and sparkled in his eyes.

"Warm enough?" he asked.

I let myself glow back at him, a smile neither coy nor cunning, but bursting with happiness. "I am warm enough."

"Then come. You shall meet Elatha."

His hand engulfed mine, and he led me down the knoll, to a pasture where wind scurried across the long grass. A massive black horse munched the green shoots, his tail swishing idly from time to time.

As Eamon and I approached the low fence, the stallion lifted his head and stared. Then he trotted toward us with a kind of dignified eagerness.

Eamon drew several chunks of carrot from his pocket. "Hold out your hand."

I spread my hand flat, as I would do when feeding any of my father's horses, and Eamon laid a piece of carrot on my palm. The horse greeted Eamon first, nuzzling against his shirt and chuffing gently, his long lashes slow-blinking over eyes as dark as Eamon's own. Then the horse turned to me, sniffing fastidiously at my hand before taking the carrot between his large lips. He looked away as he crunched it—a prince accepting the gift of a lowly vassal. I liked him at once.

"This is Elatha," said the Horseman. "Named after the Prince of Darkness, the Glory of Weapons, ruler of the Tuatha Dé Danann. My father's tales of him were always my favorite."

"The Tuatha Dé Danann are a mythical race, are they not?"

"The god-race of Ireland. Powerful beings. I have always yearned to be one of them, instead of this hellish thing." He tapped his collar. "But Fae like me are not of the Tuatha Dé Danann, nor do we have their power or their long life."

"Do any of them yet live?" Now that I knew dullahan existed, anything seemed possible. Goblins in holes, fairies in hollows—tall, beautiful gods with mystical powers and lives spanning centuries or more.

"A few may still exist. Most of them left Ireland generations ago, and the rest were slaughtered by humans. One human queen in particular, Queen Maeve, led a crusade against the Tuatha Dé Danann, and against all Fae in the land. Those that escaped her fled throughout Europe, and some came to these colonies—these states—for refuge. My ancestors were among them."

"You must tell me more about the Tuatha Dé Danann sometime." I stroked Elatha's smooth nose. His nostrils flared, but no flames or smoke issued from them as in the fireside tales of the Horseman. "Ichabod would have loved this—meeting you, discovering who you really are, learning your history." Grief knit itself tight in my throat, choking off the words.

"I am sorry for the loss of your friend." Eamon rubbed his horse's neck, his voice gruff with emotion. "But I am glad I did not have to slice off his head before your very eyes. I do not think you could ever have forgiven me for that."

"Perhaps not." I gave Elatha a final pat as he turned and trotted back into the pasture. "Can you tell me what it is like, when you change? How do you hunt down your victims?"

He braced his arms on the fence and looked down at his hands. "It is part of the magic. I am drawn to the one whose name I have been given, like a fox to the henhouse, or the tides to the shore. I simply know which direction to take, and where to find the target."

"Could they run from you? Could they simply keep running away, or fight you off somehow?"

"Unlikely. When I ride, I do not need sight to guide Elatha—he knows the lanes and forests now, so all I need to do is twitch the reins in the right direction occasionally, as I feel the tug of the magic. I usually send out my skull to survey the area, to discover the exact location of my prey and to identify any obstacles in my path." His tone turns hard and emotionless; he will not look toward me. "Once my skull is close enough to the victim, I call their name, and they are paralyzed by dullahan magic. So you see, they cannot defend themselves or flee again. Since I come upon them without warning, none of them get very far, or last very long, even if they do try to run."

I gripped the weathered rail of the fence, imagining the terror each victim must feel—helpless and frozen in place, watching their death approach. "Have you ever tried to resist the compulsion to kill?"

"A dullahan can resist for a long while if they are new to the change and have taken no heads. The more heads you have captured, the more powerful your compulsion becomes. So for someone like me, who has taken seven—"

"It is too hard to resist," I finished.

"Yes." He rubbed his forehead, still avoiding my gaze. "I did not fight Anika the first time, because she was justified in wanting her husband dead. She showed me the evidence of what he had done, and I was only too happy to help her destroy him." He sighed. "If I had known how quickly her power over me would grow, how many more she would ask me to slay—"

I laid my hand on his wrist. "You could not have known."

With another sigh, he moved closer, wrapping his enormous arm around my shoulders and pulling me to his side. I leaned gratefully into his solid warmth. "Can we stay out here all day?"

"I have work to do—firewood to chop, traps to check. And you should not be on your feet that long."

"We could bring blankets and pillows out here. I can relax under the sky, and when you're done with your work, you can come to me." I tilted my face up to his, biting my lip a little, knowing full well the effect of that expression, with my blue eyes and golden hair.

His face melted into the half-smile I loved. "Do you practice that in the mirror, Katrina?"

I let my lip go and frowned, turning away. "Perhaps."

"It is very effective, even with a 'cold-hearted eunuch' like me." The last words were delivered in a throaty male whisper right by my ear, and I could not suppress a shiver. "That was the phrase you used, wasn't it?"

"You proved me wrong." Why was I feeling so restlessly hot again? His presence tantalized and tempted me until I could scarcely think.

Then he moved away, and with the heat of his body gone, the chill of the autumn day seeped through my blanket.

"I will make you a bed outdoors," he said. "If you promise to look at me like that again, later."

I spun toward him, eager to comply, and he winked at me before striding back to the cabin.

He seemed so cheerful today, so happy. I wanted to think it was more than the release I provided for his body. Maybe I was also offering some relief for his heart. He was clearly lonely, weighed down by guilt, torn between what he wanted to accomplish with his life and what he was being forced to do. If I could soften that ache for him, even a little, it was a more worthy effort than any I had yet undertaken in my twenty years.

Eamon returned with an armful of blankets and pillows, and his enormous Horseman's coat. He spread half the blankets on the ground, tucked me under them, and draped the rest over me, with strict instructions for me to stay put.

I stayed, only changing positions when he began to chop firewood, because I was neither a nun nor a Puritan, and I was not about to miss the delicious sight of the Horseman stripped to the waist, his tanned skin glistening with sweat as he split chunks of log down the middle. The gold band at his throat flashed in the sun, and every slick ridge of his abs contracted divinely with the power of each swing.

How could Anika keep this beautiful man hidden away in the hills? Was her motive more than secrecy? Perhaps she knew that if I had ever chanced to meet him, Brom would have immediately faded to the background of my mind. What sane woman would not want a man like Eamon—collar, scythe, skull, and all?

Sighing, I tore my eyes from him for a moment and rolled over to stare at the pasture, where Elatha galloped with his head high and his tail streaming in the wind. I should not continue fooling myself with dreams and delusions. What future could there ever be for me with Eamon, while he had to serve Anika?

But I would not give him up, not if I had to climb into the hills every week by myself just to visit him. I burned for him, craved him. I wanted his voice, reading to me. His powerful hands touching me with such care. His gruff responses softened by half-smiles. The way he sliced through all my preening and affectations and unveiled my true self. The way he relished those revelations as though I were some secret treasure he had always coveted.

He was mine. The one I had been waiting for. The face I had desired, without knowing it—the like-minded soul that mine had been searching out.

The sun climbed the azure slope of the sky to its very peak. Eamon quit his labors and came to me with food—bread and apples and berry jam, and more of the soft cheese. I painted some of the jam across my mouth and pursed my lips at him.

"No, Katrina," he said, eyeing the sweet glaze on my lips.

"Why not?" I smiled a little.

"Because—ah, the devil take you." He leaned in and licked my mouth clean, his tongue teasing between my lips. "Where do you get such wicked thoughts?"

"From my own wicked mind." I tugged aside the loose fabric of my shirt, revealing most of one breast. I scooped another dollop of jam and smoothed it onto my skin, near the tip of my breast. Eamon blinked, disbelief flaring his eyes.

"Go on," I said, leaning back on my hands. "It's delicious."

"Katrina—" He glanced around us.

"There is no one but us out here," I said. "You need to have more fun."

His eyes locked with mine. "Have you ever teased anyone else like this?"

"Not this brazenly, no."

"And what we did last night—had you done that with a man?" His tone was serious—no trace of a smile.

My own grin dissolved as well. "You are the only one," I said quietly.

He put his mouth to me then, licking away the sweetness, laving my breast with his broad tongue. Then he kissed me, warm and deep, as if he were sealing a spell.

I cupped the back of his head in both my hands and yielded to the pleasure of kissing him. I teased his lips with delicate touches—flickers of tongue, sweet words whispered across his soft mouth. It was perfect and yet not enough; I opened wider to him, and his kisses turned deliriously savage. His hands swept through my hair, traveled my back—his tongue was a lash of liquid flame in my mouth. Nothing else existed except him and me, breathing and igniting and fusing together. The only spot of darkness marring our glow was the insistent pain in my back, growing stronger with each roll of my hips against his.

I opened my eyes. Somehow I was in his lap, shamelessly surging against him. I did not remember changing positions.

I stilled, biting my lip against the growing discomfort. "I need to stop."

"Of course." He carefully lifted me off him. "Are you all right?"

"Some pain."

"I'm sorry." He looked so dejected that I caught his jaw in my hand and forced him to look at me.

"We did nothing I regret," I told him. "Those kisses were worth any pain."

His remorseful expression diffused into a grin."I could kiss you like that for hours. How do people in love get any work done?"

I gasped a little, covering my mouth in playful shock. "What did you say?"

"Nothing." His face reddened and he got up, muttering something about traps and returning later.

I sank onto the blankets to rest, but my smile stayed for a good while, and returned each time I rehearsed his words in my head.

I could kiss you like that for hours.

How do people in love get any work done?

People.

In love.

I spent the afternoon soaking in the sunshine, occasionally stretching my legs and chatting to Elatha, who seemed almost as glad of my company as his master was. Far from being a hell-monster, he was a sociable animal and kept coming back to the fence to greet me.

A few times I heard the trip and tussle of small creatures in the undergrowth at the edge of the meadow. Once, after I had been lying still a while on the blankets, a rabbit hopped right past me. He leaped frantically aside when he realized that I was something alive and possibly predatory—and he skittered off into the bushes so fast that I laughed. But as he disappeared, my gaze latched on something else in the trees—a flash of movement, of something pale and tall. My heart constricted. Was someone watching me?

I stared at the spot until my eyes burned, but I saw nothing else—no sign of the shape, no additional movement. I began to doubt myself. Perhaps it was only a deer. The height and the lightness of the coloring would fit that theory. And if it had been human, surely the person would have accosted me if they recognized me—and if they did not recognize me, then why should I care if I was spotted?

Slowly I relaxed, returning to my current project—braiding together as many long grasses as possible into a perfectly useless rope.

When Eamon came back, it was late afternoon, and the sky was beginning to glow with the rosy warmth that precedes an especially beautiful sunset.

"Grab a few of the blankets," he said. "I will fetch us more food, and then there is something I want to show you."

He donned his coat and hurried to the cabin. When he came back, he carried a cloth bag, a lantern, and a waterskin. His eyes shone with purpose and eagerness. "Come with me. It's not far, and we will take it slowly."

Together we skirted the pasture fence. The trail he chose led up a gradual incline, higher into the hills. Newly fallen leaves clustered along the edges of the path in a colorful litter of scarlet and orange and gold. Above our heads, the sun streamed through the remaining foliage, turning it to incandescent fire. I felt like some princess of old, being led into Faerieland by a dark Fae prince. Of course I would have been the girl who gave up my true name easily for the promise of a dance with a beautiful devil. And I would have regretted it when the magical glitter dissolved, and the faerie sweets turned rotten and sour in my mouth.

A moment later we stepped out of the trees onto a rocky ledge high above the valley. To our right, some little way down the hillside, I spied the curling smoke from the Horseman's cabin. Spread out before us was a view the like of which I had never witnessed—golden fields, emerald pastures, fluffy clusters of amber forest speckled with dark evergreen. Far away, on the opposite side of Sleepy Hollow, the hills swept up to the sky, clad in yellow and scarlet, their smoky blue peaks yielding to a wash of clear pink sky.

Eamon set down what he carried and put his arm around me.

Silently we bathed our souls in beauty, in the clarity of the air and the scent of the wind-washed world. The tang of wood smoke curled past my nostrils, merging with the rich leather scent of Eamon's greatcoat. A blue-jay squalled from a pine tree nearby. Half-dried leaves shivered in the breeze, and though it was chilly, the firm press of Eamon's fingers around my blanketed shoulder gave me all the warmth I needed.

"I brought food," he said softly, as if the beauty around us was a live thing that might flee at a sharp word. "And I brought a book."

We spread blankets on the ledge and drank the warmth of the sinking sun while we ate. Eamon read to me from Christopher Marlowe's play *A Tragical History of the Life and Death of Doctor Faustus*—a text which I had once borrowed from a former teacher of mine, before Ichabod arrived in Sleepy Hollow. My parents were doubtful about the plot, and would not allow me to add it to our small collection of volumes.

I wondered, at first, why Eamon had the play in his possession; but as he read, I began to understand why he, a physician, and something of a demon in his own eyes, might find it compelling.

> Be a physician, Faustus; heap up gold,
> And be eternized for some wondrous cure...
> The end of physic is our body's health.
> Why, Faustus, hast thou not attained that end?
> ...Couldst thou but make men to live eternally,
> Or, being dead, raise them to life again,
> Then this profession were to be esteemed.

The demon Mephistopheles had always been my favorite character, and it was a true delight to hear his words in Eamon's deep tones.

> Why, this is Hell, nor am I out of it:
> Think'st though that I, who saw the face of God,
> And tasted the eternal joys of heaven,
> Am not tormented with ten thousand hells,
> In being deprived of everlasting bliss?

I could have listened to his sonorous voice forever. When the light faded, he lit the lantern he had brought, and we curled beneath blankets.

"Tell me more of your secrets," I whispered, tracing a finger along the bridge of his nose.

"There is a tunnel beneath the Old Church Bridge," he said. "Its entrance is concealed by a woven hanging of branches and ivy. It lets out not far from my cabin. We do not often take that route because it has a low ceiling and is therefore uncomfortable for both Elatha and I—but it has served us well a few times, when someone was getting too close and we needed to escape."

"So Lucas was right about the tunnel! But he said it led to Hell, that he saw a fiery glow."

"The glow he saw was my flaming skull, most likely—serving as our lantern as we passed through."

"Of course." I chewed my lip as I tried to recall every story I had heard of the Horseman. "Did you ever race Brom Van Brunt for a bowl of punch?"

"Ah, the boisterous Brom. I have seen him a few times since I returned here, but never at close enough range for him to recognize me. Yes, he shouted a challenge at me once, when I was out for a kill. I waved for him to go on his way, but he rode to me and spurred his horse alongside mine."

"He claims that his horse beat yours."

Eamon scoffed. "He's a fool, saving his pride by concocting a story. For all his brash talk, he came very near losing his head that night. He simply would not get out of my way, and I had to fight the magic's impulse to kill him so I could proceed with my task. Thankfully I was able to pass him after we crossed the bridge. After that, Elatha and I outdistanced him quickly."

"What about Old Brouwer? He says that you frightened his horse when he was returning from the market. You caused him to spill his coins." I ran my fingers through Eamon's hair, making it stick up even more wildly than usual. "Brouwer claims that you were planning to carry him off to the Devil."

Eamon groaned, slapping a palm to his forehead. "I remember that old fool. I was on my way to take the head of a pickpocket who stole from Anika, and my skull happened to spook old Brouwer's nag. The compulsion to leave him behind and ride for the kill was strong, but I was still lucid enough to feel bad for him—he was so feeble, and unable to walk far on his own. I thought I would take him along and drop him off near a house where he could get a ride back home. Clearly he thought I meant to kill him. He jumped straight off my saddle, over the side of the Old Church Bridge, and into the stream. It's a miracle he did not break his neck. After that incident, I vowed to myself that I would not try to help anyone while in my dullahan form."

"But you broke that vow for me."

"You were bleeding out. Dying." He moved one of my curls aside and kissed my forehead. "The way you looked at me, Katrina—the courage and desperation in your eyes—your fire burned low at the time, but I could sense it. And I could not let you die. Besides, my mission that night was fulfilled with Ichabod's death.

Had you stayed conscious a moment longer, you would have seen my head returning to my body as your schoolmaster's soul slipped away."

"Then he wasn't yet dead, when Brom threw him off the bridge." Horror twisted my stomach.

"Do not think on it." Eamon crushed his lips to mine, as if by doing so he could banish the image of Ichabod's life gurgling out of him, staining the flow of the stream.

Ichabod died alone, in the dark under the bridge.

I could hardly bear it. My very bones ached with the knowledge, with the question—could I have saved him, somehow? Reacted more quickly? Extracted the branch from his neck? No, not possible, the extent of the injury—the injury had been—this kiss of Eamon's was—warm—comforting—it was a golden cloud spreading through my body, softening the memories and muddling the questions. Even the faint thread of ever-present pain in my back disappeared in the magic of the kiss. I surrendered to it—to the whisper of his lashes against my cheek, to the brush of his scruff against my palm. His body crowded closer to mine under the blanket and I moaned my approval, plunging my hands between the stiff folds of his coat, working them down to the hardening bulge I knew I would find.

He responded in kind. His fingers wandered to the band of my trousers and slipped beneath them, diving to the spot I had shown him the other night. His touch teased slick warmth from my body and a faint whine of need from my lips.

"You are making it very hard for me to let you go tomorrow," he said thickly.

I froze. "Tomorrow?"

"I think you are well enough for a ride into the valley, if we bind your wound thickly and take it slowly." His fingers withdrew from me. "We should get you home soon."

"I don't want to go back to the valley."

"Your parents, Katrina. They are probably grieving you."

"Then they will be all the more exuberant when I finally return alive," I retorted.

"That is a selfish answer and you know it."

Exasperated, I shoved against his chest. "Are you trying to drive me away?"

"To keep you safe." His tone turned doleful. "Once you are back at home, we must never see each other again."

"Stop it. That is impossible. I cannot be apart from you, not for long."

"You are being foolish, Katrina."

"No, *you* are being foolish. You cannot make me love you and then send me back home to marry Brom. Is that what you want? Brom as my husband, hanging over me, cramming his kisses down my throat, rutting into me—"

"Stop!" Eamon clapped a hand over my mouth. "Stop. Very well, you can stay. Devil take me—you can stay as long as you want."

"Good." I pressed my cheek against his chest, listening to the rapid thump of his heart. "Then I will stay forever."

"For now," he amended. "Until you realize that you miss all the luxuries of home."

"I already miss them. But I have found something I would miss more."

His voice thrummed through his ribs into my ear. "You said something, a moment ago—that I made you love me."

"Did I?" I hid a smile in the fold of his shirt. "That does not sound like something Katrina the Coquette would say."

"It does not," he conceded. "But Katrina the Tender-Hearted and Compassionate, Katrina the Clever and Quick-Tongued, Katrina the Irresistible—she might have said it."

"Katrina the Irresistible," I crooned, lifting my face to his. "I think I like it. You must call me that again sometime."

We lay there a long while, sheltered beneath a latticework of whispers and promises—as if words could protect us from the savage world. As if the quiet night could go on forever, and reality would wait as long as we needed it to. As if our kisses had the power to stop time.

"Should we go back?" I whispered at last. "I'm a little cold, and the ground is hard."

"Of course." He leaped up at once, packing up our supplies. I rolled the blankets, moving carefully so as not to disturb my wound.

"Katrina, you should look at the valley," Eamon said. "It is so beautiful in the evening, with all the lighted windows."

"Just a moment." I tightened the blanket roll.

A sharp clapping of broad wings and a faint squawk startled me.

I turned my head in time to see Eamon untwist a scrap of something from the leg of a hawk I recognized. Brom's hawk, brown-feathered with wingtips as black as the night itself.

Horror shuddered in my throat—I wanted to scream, to tell him to stop—but he unrolled the paper before I could make a sound. Words floated from his lips—phrases spoken tonelessly in an unfamiliar tongue, ending with three words I knew all too well—"Katrina Van Tassel."

Eamon looked at me, his lips parted and his eyes already glazed with fell purpose.

The band around his throat glowed brighter and brighter. It dissolved from his neck and floated in a cloud of golden sparks, reforming in his hand as a shining scythe with a wickedly sharp blade.

"Katrina." His voice rasped from his throat between ragged breaths. "Run from me. Run!" The last word climbed into a groaning shriek as his neck jerked aside with a hideous snap. The skin stretched and separated, tendons popping free—and then his head tore away from his body. His beautiful face sizzled, splitting into fiery cracks that branched and widened as flames consumed his skin. Flakes of flesh, black as ash, fell away like shed scales, until nothing was left but raw white bone licked with gold and orange fire. Dark smoke streamed from the stump of his neck, like wild hair tossed on the wind.

The Thing before me was no longer Eamon. It was human-shaped, yet sickeningly wrong—a denizen of the uncanny valley, dripping with the horror of the Other and the Unmade.

The dullahan.

The Headless Horseman.

6

The flaming skull darted toward me, opening its skeletal jaws.

"I cannot hold back for long." Its voice was vaguely Eamon's, but gravelly and echoing, like a demon roaring from some far-off pit of Hell. "Run!"

Even as the skull spoke to me, the Horseman's massive arm lifted, brandishing the golden scythe. But he did not speak my name. He did not freeze me in place and render me helpless—though he stalked toward me, slow and heavy, drawn to me like a compass needle is sucked toward True North.

No spell had sealed me in place when he read my name from the note; but if he spoke it again, I would be paralyzed.

I fled.

No time to think about the sharp twinges of pain in my back. Fear fueled my steps, and I bounded along the path like a deer, terrified and trembling.

A thought formed, clear and sure. I had to get to Elatha before the Horseman did. The stallion was my only chance of survival.

The sunlight had faded, and stars glinted like teeth through the dark limbs of the trees. No gateway to Faerieland here, and no stately columns crested with glittering colors. That illusion was shredded by shadows, and the trees tunneled around the pathway, closing me in.

My toe caught on the edge of a rock and I nearly fell; but I lurched forward, risking one look over my shoulder.

My Horseman stalked me, a dread hunter with a skull of bone and fire. As I stared with sick fascination, his head darted forward, streaming flames, a smoky hiss issuing from its mouth and echoing between the shrouded trees.

I clapped my hands over my ears, and I ran again. Faster this time. My feet pounded over hard-packed earth, their frantic beat dulled by the layer of dead leaves. Down the slope I raced, so fast I nearly tumbled in a headlong slurry of rotten leaves and panic. I slowed as much as I dared, so as not to spook the stallion who stood ahead of me in the center of the field, his head lifted to the wind. He seemed more alert now, and restive. Maybe he could smell the hellish smoke from the Horseman's skull.

Even as I had the thought, the skull blazed over my head, showering sparks. They winked out before they touched the dry grass.

With a tiny shriek I leaped forward, calling to the horse in a breathy, overly cheerful voice. "Elatha! Elatha, come here. Come to me."

The skull whirled up into the sky, screeching something that sounded like my name, only garbled, with the syllables scattered in the wrong places.

Eamon was fighting the fell sway of his magic. He was straining against it, for me, so I would have a chance to escape.

"Elatha," I crooned to the horse again.

If only I had a treat, something to tempt him. But apparently he remembered the carrots from earlier in the day, and our interludes of conversation—he trotted toward me, ears tilted forward with interest.

I had nothing to use for a saddle or bridle. I took a handful of his mane, cupped his face with my arm, and led him toward the fence.

We reached it just as the Horseman himself marched out of the forest. His scythe caught the icy starlight as he swished it, back and forth, back and forth, the blade whipping low to the ground, slicing the longest of the grasses.

Biting back another scream, I stepped onto the fence and launched myself onto Elatha's back. Agony bit into my wound, but I felt no rush of blood. Even if I had, this was no time to worry about it.

I pressed my knees and calves to the horse as tightly as I could and took two fistfuls of mane. Quick and light, I tapped my heels to Elatha's sides—not to hurt him, but to send the message *go, go, go.*

He hesitated.

"Elatha." My voice cracked with urgency. "Please. Go!"

The stallion wheeled and galloped across the field, away from the Horseman. We rode fast, approaching the fence at a pace that chilled my blood—I clenched my legs for dear life, sobbing with pain and fear.

A hideous floating sensation—my stomach sailed into my throat—then a crash of hooves on the ground, and we were safely over the pasture fence and off again.

I guided Elatha as best I could, steering him downhill as much as possible. I had no idea where Eamon's shortcut tunnel was, and I could not spare the time to search for it. As long as the horse and I were headed into the valley, toward buildings and people, I'd have a chance. I was moving much faster than Eamon—he would have to walk the entire distance that Elatha and I covered.

We found a path, of a sort—a passable swath of space between the clustering trees. Elatha must have traveled it before on his forays with the Horseman. As he cantered down, down, toward the valley, I had a chance to breathe, and to think.

Anika had been at the cabin today. It must have been her I glimpsed in the woods, watching me. Perhaps she had come to give Eamon new orders, or to bring him something—or perhaps she had not fully believed his explanation during her first visit. She had seen me lying outside, and realized that I knew more than I should about her dullahan murder-slave. And she had decided that I must die.

My fate was sealed.

A dullahan never stopped pursuing its victim. Once given a name, it must capture the victim's head, or remain headless forever. Unless—

Eamon had told me he was magically prevented from killing his Ceannaire or her family members. Unable to free himself that way, he said.

So perhaps slaying a dullahan's Ceannaire could free him. But could it undo the kill order he was most recently given?

If I killed Anika Van Brunt, would I be saved? Or would Eamon still have to slay me—one final act before he was set free?

Tears flew past my cheeks as I smiled into the dark. Did it matter? If I died in the freeing of one enslaved soul, surely the sacrifice would be worthwhile. After all, I was a spoiled, selfish coquette, and Eamon was a trained physician, dedicated to helping the least fortunate. If only one of us could survive the night, it should be him. He was worth ten—no, twenty—of me.

But Anika—soft, dimpled, laughing Anika. Like a second mother to me. A friend, or so I had thought. Could I really kill her? End her, with my own hands? I looked down at them, thin white fingers twisted desperately into the rough locks of Elatha's mane.

It is a terrible sorrow, taking a life.

Anika Van Brunt had planned my father's murder. She intended to kill him after my wedding to Brom. She had killed others, appointed herself the executioner of every petty thief or suspicious vagrant who entered Sleepy Hollow.

Maybe her first kill had been justified, but not the others. Not the past murders, the ones she had commanded Eamon to commit, and not the future killings she would force him into. Sweet, noble, compassionate Eamon, stricken and spelled into whacking off the heads of any human Anika deemed unworthy.

I could not allow it to stand.

For him, I would do this terrible thing. I would carry the guilt and the sorrow. I had killed one innocent man by accident; I could kill a guilty woman with clear intent.

A sharp yell sounded from the forest, and I jumped so hard I nearly tumbled from Elatha's back. I righted myself, but something swept past my head, and I screamed. Not a fiery skull—this thing was dark and feathered. An owl, most likely. Elatha, bless him, was used to screams and shocks—he did not falter, or toss me off.

    We struck a road then—a road that I knew. The road that led over the Old Church Bridge.

    From here, I could direct Elatha to Brom's house. I guided him to the right, away from my house and toward the Van Brunts' farm. Elatha slowed, cantering along, and I let him set the pace while I fretted.

    Brom would likely not be at home this evening. After the day's work, he often went out carousing with his companions, to play pranks or cards, or to drink at the ramshackle building that doubled as inn and pub together. Sometimes they rode to another village, to see new faces and bosoms, and to try new ales.

    I prayed to God that Brom would be away. If he was in the house, I would have no chance to—to kill—I could scarcely even think the words.

    Never mind the prayers. Why would God have an interest in helping me commit a murder? Even if I was doing it to free a man, and to possibly avoid more murders—even then I could not expect divine blessing on the act.

    Even if Brom were not at the farm, I would have difficulty with Anika. She knew that I knew about

Eamon, or she would not have made me his next target. If I confronted her, there was every chance she would try to kill me herself, or hold me captive until the Horseman arrived to finish me off.

When we came to the lane leading to Brom's house, I slid off Elatha's back and left him in the shadow of a tree before slipping through the gate. Brom's dog Wodan—a savage, nearly feral beast that would bite off the hand of anyone who tried to pet him—streaked across the grass toward me, straight as an arrow. He never barked, which made him all the more deadly.

The first time I met Wodan, he had nearly launched himself at my throat. Brom had stopped him with an outthrust arm to the beast's chest. Then Brom stroked my hands and patted my arms until the dog realized I was a friend, not a threat. As the final step in our introduction, Brom had given me a chunk of raw meat to feed to the dog.

Since then, Wodan had never threatened me, as long as I let him approach and sniff me before I proceeded to the house—and as long as I made no attempt to touch him.

Wodan stopped just short of me and put his nose to the ground, running it along until it touched my foot. He growled deep in his throat and took a long time sniffing me over, probably because I carried the scent of the Horseman and his steed.

"I do not have time for this, you abominable brute," I said in my sweetest, softest tones. "It's Katrina, Wodan. You know me."

Finally the dog sneezed once and trotted away along the fence. Inhaling deeply to fortify myself, I walked toward the Van Brunt's farmhouse.

I had known this house all my life. It was perhaps half the size of ours, in decent repair, although Brom sometimes neglected its upkeep in favor of his own pursuits. I knew that the front steps creaked and the back door squeaked, that Anika Van Brunt's room was at the top of the stairs, but that she was likely to be in the parlor at this hour, sewing and humming to herself, or reading and stroking the cat, who was as fluffy as a pillow and not much of a mouser. The thought of Anika sewing and plotting death, and smiling over her cat while others fled through the woods in terror of the Horseman—it spurred another surge of bile in my stomach. For a moment I thought I would be sick; but I breathed again, drawing in cold night air through my nose, and the urge receded.

I chose the front door as my place of entry, avoiding the steps entirely by hauling myself straight up to the porch. It wrenched my back to do it, but my stitches appeared to hold.

If Brom was not at home, the front door would be unlatched to admit him when he returned. He did not like to go in by the back if he could help it. As the master of the house, he thought a rear entrance was too good for him.

Gently I tried the door, and it opened easily.

So Brom was out for the evening. I allowed myself a small sigh of relief as I stepped inside and eased the door shut behind me.

The front room lay empty, dark, and silent, like a tomb awaiting bodies to fill it. The Van Brunts had a couple of laborers who lived at the back of the property, but they would not return to the main house tonight. Anika and I would not be interrupted.

As quietly as I could, I slipped off my shoes and padded on bare feet toward the parlor. A slash of flickering golden light shone from that doorway, splitting the indigo darkness of the front room. A rhythmic creak and the faint crackle of a low fire sifted into the dark as well—sounds that should mean comfort, and peace, and safety. Instead they sounded like death omens, and set my heart thrumming faster.

Softly, softly I crept closer, careful to avoid the squeaky places in the floor. Brom and I used to make a game of sneaking up on our mothers while they were tête-à-tête in the parlor, gossiping over tea and needlework. Strange that such a game could mean life or death to me now.

One foot here. Another there. Now a step toward the wall. Slowly, softly—yet hurry, hurry, because I had lost time waiting for the dog to go away, and I had lost time easing the front door open, and I lost yet more time taking off my shoes. The Horseman might be supernaturally quick on his feet. He might have taken the shortcut tunnel and thus saved himself time, while Elatha and I took the long, slow path. He might be at the gate even now, his deadly instinct drawing him to me.

If Eamon did kill me, he would never recover from the horror of it. Of that, I had no doubt.

My brain conjured the image of my beautiful Horseman coming back to himself after the kill, seeing my severed head—would he roar with agony, or weep silently? Neither, if I had my way.

I peered into the parlor. Anika sat in her rocker, with her back to me, watching the fire. The angle of the rocker allowed me a glimpse of the cat on her lap. Her work-creased hand drifted over its snowy fur with such a gentle touch, the way she used to stroke my hair when I was little.

Anika. My aching heart breathed her name. She was like family. And yet she had ordered the Horseman to kill me. Did she feel guilty over it? Was she mourning for me now, sitting there in her rocker, staring into the fireplace?

No sooner had the thought crossed my mind than she sighed and murmured, "Oh, Katrina, Katrina. You stupid, stupid girl. God have mercy on your soul."

I did not have to look to my left; I knew exactly where the heavy pewter pitcher sat on the glossy china cabinet beside me. I gripped it, switching it to my right hand, and advanced, raising it, my heart booming like a cannon in my chest, so loud that she must hear it—

Perhaps the cat heard it. He slid smoothly from Anika's lap, bounding away into a shadowy corner. Anika sighed but remained motionless, with her hands upturned and limp in her lap.

I must do this, to save Eamon. I must.

I clutched the pitcher tighter, and swung it in a savage arc toward Anika's temple.

The pewter rang against her skull, a horrible hollow sound that sickened me. She did not scream, but fell forward out of the chair, gasping and scrambling away, pressing a hand to her temple. Her fingers came away bloody.

Then she looked at me. In her eyes shone the dread that Doctor Faustus must have felt when Mephistopheles came for his soul.

"Katrina!" My name escaped her mouth in a sob of fear and anger. "You cannot be here. You will draw him to my house—you cannot—"

"How could you?" Rage traveled my veins, sudden and hot, giving me a fierce, wicked strength. "You were like my mother's sister. Like my second mother."

"It has to be done. And you have to leave." She lurched to her feet, wavering, and turned her back to me. She staggered nearer to the fire; but before she could seize the poker and strike me, I darted forward and locked my arm across her throat, as I had seen Brom do countless times to boys who annoyed him. He always let go before the lack of breath became too perilous, and his victims were left with a bruise and a better respect for him.

But I must not let go. I must show no mercy. I must see it through until the end, until the flight of Anika's soul.

I braced the chokehold with my other hand, tightening my grip, grinding my forearm into her throat as fiercely as I could. The frantic strength that had buoyed me this night was ebbing, weakening—soon I would start shaking and I would collapse, entirely spent.

"I'm sorry," I gasped. "I'm sorry, I'm sorry."

Anika's fingers scrabbled at my arms. Then she raked at my face, but I turned it aside, shutting my eyes tight.

"I have to." The words rushed from me in a sob. "If only you could have left him alone—left us alone—forgive me."

She bucked, throwing us both backward. I crashed against the wall, and agony flared in my back, but I held on. Tighter. Tighter. Power and clenched teeth and raw bone-deep determination.

Then the front steps squalled and creaked.

The door of the house splintered and smashed under rhythmic, heavy blows.

Anika's hands were flailing limply now. She was going lax in my arms. Passed out, but not dead. Not yet.

The stamp of the Horseman's boots drummed through the front room.

Fiercely I crushed Anika's throat, praying to someone, anyone, to snatch her soul away before the Horseman reached me. Before he lifted that golden scythe and sliced through my neck—skin and tendons and bone and jetting blood—my life, spewing and streaming away, my soul whisked off to—

—to Hell, surely.

I could endure Hell, if I knew that Eamon was free. If I had hope that one day he might be there too. Strange thoughts, muddled and nonsensical, born of exhaustion and of terror because *there he was*, my Horseman, a hulking figure in the doorway.

His skull skimmed into the room, two grinning rows of teeth and a couple of blazing eye sockets. "Katrina Van Tassel."

The name curled around my limbs, locking them in place. I could not even say his name, or remind him what I hoped I meant to him, what we were becoming together.

He lifted the scythe. Swept it outward in an arc.

And then he paused, his arm shaking.

His skull whisked near me, its heat singeing my lashes and brows. "Katrina..." The voice from those jaws was stone and agony, chains and wretchedness.

Then—a sharp whirr through the air as the skull was sucked backward, away from me. Back toward him.

No pain seared the tender skin of my neck. No slicing blade cleaved my head from my body.

The Horseman's skull settled between his shoulders with a faint crack of reconnected spine. The fire tightened around the facial bones, glowing, changing, metamorphosing into flesh and skin and black hair. The golden scythe dissolved, floating in glittering remnants up to his neck, where it reformed and locked in place— the collar, complete with its row of terrible runes.

The spell around me vanished. I could move again, and move I did, pushing Anika off me. Her body had released its contents—her skirts were soaked and reeking. She was truly dead.

And I was alive.

And Eamon was free.

7

Eamon stared at me, his lips trembling. "Katrina..."

I struggled to my feet. "She cannot hurt anyone else now. Eamon—forgive me—" I swayed, pitching forward. Eamon caught me and swung me up in his arms. "We have to go," he whispered. "No one can find us here."

"My shoes—I left them by the front door—"

"We will fetch them."

I did not remember much of the ride back to the cabin. When we reached it, Eamon checked my wound and told me that the stitches still held well enough, despite a little seepage of blood.

We spent the next day wrapped together and bundled in blankets, moving only when our bodies needed food, or drink, or relief. It was a necessary cocoon of physical comfort, a recovery from the terror we had both endured.

We barely spoke throughout the long day.

At last, when evening came, I tucked my face into Eamon's shoulder and whispered to him, told him how I felt while he was chasing me, what I thought during the reckless ride to the Van Brunt's farm, how I had found Anika, how certain I was that I would die before I managed to free him. How I wasn't sure that her death would allow him to spare me.

"I fought it, Katrina, with everything I had." His voice was raw, agonized. "The power of the collar—the compulsion I labor under in that form—I couldn't resist it, not for long. I'm sorry."

"I know." I kissed him. "Eamon, I want to know if you think differently of me, now that I've killed someone—not from any compulsion, but of my own free will. I did it for you—for myself—for Anika's future victims—but still, I took a life. Can you ever look at me the same way?"

In answer he kissed me soundly, then stroked my hair, letting its golden strands slide through his fingers. "You are the fiercest friend I have ever had. I love you, and nothing you have done or will do can ever change that."

Something unlocked inside me then. Every love in my life had been conditional—dependent on my behavior, my eligibility, my wealth, my position, my pious attitude, my beauty, my performance as a daughter.

Eamon had seen me wounded, wretched, dirty, disheveled, irreverent, murderous—and still he loved me.

I pushed myself up on my elbow in the bed. "That does it. I am going to marry you."

"What?" He half-smiled. "Are you joking?"

"Not at all."

"But—I have nothing. I am not the man your parents would want for you."

"I have plenty for both of us. And you have your training as a physician. Dr. Burton is getting old and rheumatic—you will have no lack of patients, if you want them."

"But will those patients want *me*, when they find out that I treat everyone, no matter the color of their skin?"

"If they do not want your excellent services, they can go die in a ditch," I snapped.

Eamon laughed, a full, rich sound straight from his belly. "I love you."

"Of course you do." But my cocky smile faded immediately, and tears gathered in my eyes. "I am so glad you do."

The next day we went down into the valley together. Lucas was the first to see us approaching on Elatha. The open joy in his face brought a smile to mine.

"Miss Katrina." He grinned up at me. "You are alive, after all. Everyone will be glad to hear it. Your mother—she's in a bad way."

I could imagine so, what with her daughter's assumed death closely followed by the death of her best friend. My heart pummeled my ribs as I slid carefully off Elatha into Eamon's arms. Mentally I ran through the story we had rehearsed—as simple and as close to the truth as possible.

"I'll walk her up to the house." Eamon nodded to Lucas. "I can see to the horse myself, if you're busy."

Lucas lifted a brow at the unexpected courtesy. "No trouble, sir. Happy to take care of such a fine animal."

"Thank you." Eamon offered me his arm.

I recognized my father's portly figure when we were still many paces from the house. His arm was lifted, crooked in its customary position when he was indulging in a pipe of tobacco.

"Papa," I breathed, and though we were too far away for him to hear me, I saw him turn toward us, and lower his arm. The next second he was shouting for my mother, and running. My father, Baltus Van Tassel, was running. I had never seen him run.

I could not run without pain, but I walked faster. As we neared each other, my father drew up short, most likely because he had noticed I was wearing a man's clothes.

"Katrina." The joy in his eyes mingled with horror at all the improprieties I was currently committing. If he only knew...

"Papa." I embraced him.

His arms tightened around me briefly before he pushed me to arm's length again. "Where have you been?"

"I was hurt on the bridge, Papa, the night Ichabod was killed. This traveling doctor found me and helped me recover."

"Why did he not send word where you were?"

"I was too injured to be left alone. I nearly died."

"This man—" Papa inspected Eamon from head to toe. Eamon had worn his best clothes, complete with a ruffled shirt, waistcoat, and cravat. He did look fine, and broad, and powerful. Even without a hint of wealth about him—no watch, or hat, or walking stick—he cut an imposing figure. Papa cleared his throat. "Well then—come inside, before people talk. We must get you into some suitable clothes, and call Dr. Burton. Young man, you will stay for dinner."

We had barely reached the porch when my mother came screaming out of the house and flung her arms around me.

"Careful!" I exclaimed. "I am still injured."

"Injured? My darling, who hurt you?" She squinted at Eamon. "Was it *you*?"

"No, Mother! He is a doctor. He has a cabin in the hills. He mended my wound, and nursed me back to health."

"Nursed you back to health, did he indeed? Hurry inside. You cannot be seen in this state, with this stranger—there are ruffians about, Katrina. We thought you had been killed, my love! And I must tell you—it will be a terrible shock to you—Anika Van Brunt has been murdered. Some craven thief smashed down the door of her house and strangled her." My mother was shaking and panting, her face pale and clammy.

Eamon reached for her just as she collapsed in a dead faint. He caught her and said to my father, "With your permission?"

Papa nodded, and Eamon carried my mother inside to a sofa.

After that gentlemanly act of his, and the medical attention he provided my mother over the next hour or so, there were no further questions about his honor—at least until I returned from dressing and came to my mother's side. She shooed everyone else out of the room, and with her hands writhing in her handkerchief, she said, "Did he do anything wicked to you, this young doctor?"

Oh yes. He did very wicked things.

"I am still a virgin," I told her.

She released an enormous breath. "Oh my child. Thank God for that. Better to be dead than defiled."

I pinched my lips to keep back a sharp retort about how I would much rather be alive in any case, and how wrong she was to think that my worth as a woman was linked to a particular orifice of my body—but my mother was a woman of rigid opinions, and no amount of talk would sway her, especially on such matters.

When Dr. Burton came, he grudgingly praised the work Eamon had done on my wound, but he suggested I stay in bed for a week or two. Mercifully, that advice excused me from Anika Van Brunt's funeral, and from seeing anyone I did not wish to encounter. Eamon could not come every day, but he visited thrice a week, according to our plan—slowly working his way into my family. His gruff, logical way of talking endeared him to my father, while his looks and training quickly gained him my mother's favor. My parents began to realize almost at once that his interest in me went beyond my physical health; and though they did not proclaim themselves in favor of his attention, they did not forbid it either.

Three weeks after my return home, I was sitting primly under the elm tree with Eamon while he read to me from *A Tragical History of the Life and Death of Doctor Faustus*. This time, it was the lines from Doctor Faustus that seemed to strip my heart naked as he read.

"Her lips suck forth my soul: see, where it flies!
Come, Helen, come, give me my soul again.
Here will I dwell, for heaven is in these lips,
And all is dross that is not Helena.

> I will be Paris, and for love of thee,
> Instead of Troy, shall Wertenberg be sack'd;
> And I will combat with weak Menelaus,
> And wear thy colours on my plumed crest;
> Yea, I will wound Achilles in the heel,
> And then return to Helen for a kiss.
> O, thou art fairer than the evening air
> Clad in the beauty of a thousand stars;
> Brighter art thou than flaming Jupiter—"

I laid my hand across the pages so Eamon was forced to stop reading. "Eamon, it is time."

"Time?" He lifted his dark eyes to mine.

"Time for you to ask for my hand in marriage. You should request my father's blessing first."

He stared down at the book, where my fingers splayed over the page, and he ran one broad fingertip up the slim central bone of my hand, all the way to my wrist. "Katrina, I do not know how to tell you this—but I think perhaps our original plan was flawed."

My stomach dropped with a sickening jerk, and I snatched my fingers away. "What do you mean?"

"I cannot ask for your hand in marriage."

This was not happening. Could not be happening.

"But—you said—you and I—"

"As I recall it, you have already proposed marriage to *me*." His mouth inched up at one side. "And I have not yet answered your proposal."

I snatched the book from his hands and struck the side of his head with it. "You cruel fiend. You absolute monster! I thought you were serious."

"But I am!" He stole the book back, tossed it aside, and captured my hands. "I owe you an answer, Katrina—but first, do you realize what marriage to me would mean? I am dullahan. I am vulnerable to anyone who might discover my secret and bind me for evil work. And our children—if we should have any—would also be dullahan, because the curse passes to the children even when human blood is introduced. Our children would carry that dreadful secret from the moment of their birth. Do you understand how the secrecy will complicate your life? Are you sure you are ready for this burden?"

I extricated one of my hands and laid my palm against his face. "I am ready. I have had weeks to think it over, and I might have a solution."

He drew away warily. "I am not going to like it, am I?"

"Do you know the ritual for binding a dullahan to a human master?"

"I do."

"Then you'll do it with me. I will be your Ceannaire, your safeguard. As long as I live, no one will be able to command you to do murder again. I can do the same for any children we may have. I will be their shield, and yours."

He rose abruptly, pacing the grass. "That puts a death mark on you. If anyone discovered our secret and wanted my power, they would kill you first."

"*If* they found out that I was your Ceannaire. And should that happen, you'd be there to protect me. We will protect each other."

"I don't know."

"I understand that you are hesitant to trust another human with this bond," I said gently. "The last time you trusted someone, it did not work out well. But I would never command you to kill anyone—never, Eamon. You have to believe that."

He rushed back to me, and for a moment I thought he would kiss me—something we had to do discreetly, if at all. But he only said, low and terse, "That is not why I hesitate. I trust you, Katrina. I trust your heart. And I do not want to put that precious heart of yours in any more danger. You cannot be my Ceannaire."

I crossed my arms. "Then I will not wed you. I withdraw my offer of marriage."

His brows drew together in a thunderous frown. "You cannot withdraw it."

"I can. The offer of marriage is revoked until you agree to let me protect you."

"Katrina..." His frustrated growl delighted me, and the swears that followed were even better.

"Such sweet music to my ears," I crooned. "Please, do continue. You have been so very civilized of late—I miss the unfettered Eamon of the cabin. When can we go back there? There are things I want to do to you." I blinked slowly at him.

"When we are married," he said through gritted teeth.

"What a pity we cannot marry until you agree to my terms."

"I will not be played with, Katrina, or forced into a decision. When we marry, this will be an equal partnership. You and I, together."

"Then you must let me protect you in my way, as you wish to defend me in yours."

I had him there; I saw the change in his face.

He stalked in a swift circle, beat his palm against the elm's trunk a few times.

"Very well," he said tightly.

"Very well? What might that mean?"

"I will marry you."

"You sound so elated." I rose from the blanket, shaking out my skirts. "Be careful, you might burst from pure happiness."

I swept past him, my chin in the air, but he caught my wrist and dragged me back. One broad hand pressed the small of my back, and his mouth claimed mine, hot and urgent. He devoured my lips, searched me out with his tongue; he stole my breath and possibly my soul—left me flushed and tingling and *wanting, wanting.*

"I have missed you," he breathed in my ear, under the fall of my curls. "I miss seeing you, lying there in my bed, or walking around in my clothes. I miss your constant questions, and your clever quips, and your incessant wickedness. I want my hands on your skin. I want to be inside you, Katrina, to be part of you. The thought of belonging to you frightens me and thrills me. I am elated to be your husband."

He pulled back, a triumphant half-smile on his face. I swallowed, scarcely able to look at him, or to stand properly.

"I want your word on a certain matter, however," he said, tracing my knuckle with his thumb. "You must promise me that when you feel trapped, as if you must burst out of your own skin, you will not hurt yourself. Instead, you can squeeze my hand very tightly. I will understand the sign, and I will immediately devise an escape for you."

"You would do that? Even if I needed to leave in the middle of a service, or avoid a quilting session with the goodwives, or run away into the woods for a while?"

"Anything you need, whenever you need it."

The sweetness of his commitment overcame me so much I could barely mouth the words. "I promise."

"Good." He kissed my fingertips. "I am going to ask your father now."

As he walked away, I fell limply back onto the blanket, clutching my shawl around me and wondering what I had done to deserve such a man. I did nothing, truthfully. I had simply been Katrina—selfish yet affectionate, sour and sweet by turns, devoted to doing right by my fellow humans, yet also decidedly immoral when it came to a certain handsome dullahan. A world of contradictions in one woman, and Eamon did not seem to mind at all.

He wanted me. All of me.

Our interludes of late had been so infrequent—and observed so closely by my parents, and the laborers, and any passing neighbors—that the idea of having him all to myself for a lifetime brought tears to my eyes. I could not bear it if my father refused. If he denied his blessing, I would leave Sleepy Hollow with Eamon and marry him elsewhere. Nothing could keep us apart—no human or angel or devil from Hell, and no curse-begotten collar of magical servitude. I had killed for Eamon already. I swore to myself, with my hand on *Doctor Faustus*, that I would leave no sin undone if it meant that he would be mine.

My father did give his blessing; though truthfully, if Eamon had not been a physician, I do not think he would have allowed it. My mother was reluctant to relinquish her dream of Brom and me, but it was difficult to resist Eamon's low voice and quiet courtesy, or to deny his medical skill. And his face—well. The beautiful dark eyes had an eloquence of their own when he told my mother how much he loved me.

Once my mother and father agreed to a thing, they plunged into its execution with their hearts and their coin-purses open. They planned a feast to celebrate the engagement—a feast that dwarfed all feasts ever held in Sleepy Hollow—a feast to which every neighbor for miles around was invited, from one end of the valley to the other.

It was a glorious affair, with more pastries and roasted meats and delectable dishes than that fateful quilting party. Ichabod's eyes would have popped from his head at the sight of such sumptuous fare. I trailed slowly along the tables, plate in hand, finding it all suddenly unappetizing. Not a dish was present that did not remind me of the skinny schoolmaster and his heaping helpings, and the relish with which he attacked his meals—and the blood-slicked spike of wood piercing through his throat.

Nausea roiled in my stomach. I set down my plate and walked away, fighting the urge to lift my knuckle to my mouth and bite it until it bled. Instead I walked to Eamon's side, where he stood talking of governments and wars with the men of the valley. I took his hand and squeezed it as hard as I could.

"If you'll excuse me, gentlemen," he said abruptly, cutting off one man in the middle of his complaints about the President.

Their startled mumblings pursued us as Eamon led me out the back door of the house and away from a crew of gamboling children, to the shadow of a tall hedgerow. Frost bit the inside of my nose, but even its freshness could not cure the horror curdling my insides.

"Breathe," Eamon said, tucking aside wisps of hair that had escaped from my coiled braids. "Breathe deep and slow."

I tried, but my stomach revolted, and I heaved its meager contents into the grass. My face burned with shame, and my throat with acid, but Eamon only rubbed my back and murmured, "That's it. Get it all out. Is that better?"

"A little."

He gave me his handkerchief to wipe my mouth. "I was sick after every kill."

"You were?"

"Yes." He wrapped an arm around me and walked me a little distance from the soiled spot. Our shoes crunched against the dry brown grass. "Do you want to talk about what troubled you?"

"Ichabod," I said slowly. "The way he used to love feasts and parties. He ate so much food, Eamon. Plates and plates of it. I can't eat from those tables without thinking of him."

"I see. What if I made you some toast? Might you be able to stomach that?"

"I think so."

"Then consider it done. I'll find you a seat first."

He escorted me indoors and installed me in a cushioned chair in the parlor. I tried to smile at the other women in the room, but I knew that my pallor and weakness would only feed the gossip mill. They were probably already convinced that I was with child.

One of the women scooted her own chair nearer to mine. "Feeling poorly, are you, dear?"

"A little."

"Where did your handsome doctor go? He should take care of you," she simpered.

"He is going to make me some toast."

She laughed, her hand fluttering to her heart. "How very odd! You have servants for that."

"He likes to do things himself."

"Indeed. You must tell us more about him."

"Yes, do," chimed in another.

"We're all so curious," added a third.

A movement in the doorway caught my eye—Sascha, beckoning to me. I seized the chance gratefully. "Excuse me, ladies."

I walked out of the room with as much dignity as I could muster.

Sascha huddled against the wall outside the parlor, holding something in her skirts. "Can we go to your room? I have something to show you."

"Of course." I led her upstairs to my bedroom and shut the door. "What is it?"

She drew out Ichabod's well-worn volume of Cotton Mather's writings. "I went to Hans Van Ripper's house, after Ichabod—after he disappeared. Brom told everyone he was killed by the Headless Horseman, but I wasn't sure, so I thought I would go and see if—" She hesitated, closing her eyes and breathing deep. "Van Ripper told me that Gunpowder had galloped home with Ichabod's saddlebag, and he said he was going to go through Ichabod's things, since he was surely dead. I told him Ichabod might yet return, but Van Ripper would not listen to me, the greedy old goat. He would have burned this book, but I managed to steal it away. It is only slightly singed, here, along the spine. I—I thought you might want it, to remember Ichabod. You two were—well, you—"

"We were friends. Thank you, Sascha." I accepted the volume, rubbing the sooty marks on the spine. Touching the book soothed me in a way I did not expect. "You liked him too, did you not?"

Sascha bit her lip, tears glistening in her eyes.

I laid my hand on her arm. "You should keep this book. It will mean more to you, I think. But you must promise me you will never get rid of it. This particular copy—it's special."

She nodded.

"Give me a moment with it, would you? I'll leave it on the bed when I'm done, and you can take it with you when you leave."

With another nod, Sascha slipped out of my room.

I carried the book to my writing table and laid it open. I rarely wrote anything—I preferred reading or being outdoors—but my mother kept the inkstand full and a fresh quill ready, in case I should decide to be a proper lady and write a letter to some relative or other.

Carefully I turned the pages, until I found the one with the notes about the dullahan. There were other notations too, throughout the tome—bits about kelpies, and selkies, and pixies, and tricksters in red coats. But the notes about the dullahan were the most copious of all.

I found a scrap of empty space in one of the margins. Dipping the quill, I wrote in my smallest, finest script. "A dullahan may not kill his own master. But another may kill the master for him, thus setting the dullahan free. If the dullahan is out hunting when the master is killed, the intended victim will be spared."

I could not be sure that anyone would ever read or need the information. But what was knowledge, without someone to pass it on?

The act of making the notation, small as it was, quelled my distress. Ichabod would have been so excited about the information, so glad of its presence in his book. This tome, this treasure of his would live on, and possibly find a soul who would truly understand its value.

Leaving the book on the bed, I stepped out of my room and leaned against the wall, closing my eyes for a moment. Saying goodbye to Ichabod.

Then I descended the stairs—only to find Brom at its foot.

His black suit of clothes hung wrinkled and slovenly from his big frame. The puffiness around his eyes spoke of late nights and frequent excessive drink.

The last time I had seen him, he was striking Ichabod, kicking him—dumping him off the side of the Old Church Bridge. He had run away and left me at the mercy of the Horseman.

Those memories turned my skin hot with anger; but I could not help being nervous too. There was no one else in the back hall, and Brom looked anything but sober.

"Brom," I said stiffly.

"Katrina."

"I am sorry you lost your mother. That must be very difficult for you."

"Yes, yes. Very difficult. I lost her, and I lost my intended bride. One fell swoop, as they say." He stepped forward and swayed, catching himself against the railing. "I hear you're getting married to some strange traveling medicine man."

"Traveling doctor," I corrected.

"They also say you spent days in this doctor's cabin." He smothered a hiccup. "You finally had some fun, eh, Katrina? You were always a greedy little whore."

The heat in my face intensified, more so because he was not entirely wrong. My desire had always been there, strong yet unfocused, an urge that many in this valley would consider unwomanly or sinful. Now my lust had found its focus, and it had merged with a love so intense that sometimes I thought my heart would burst with the fullness of it.

I had nothing to be ashamed of.

"You should leave, Brom," I said. "You are too drunk to recall your manners."

He mounted two steps, unexpectedly fast for someone so inebriated, and my skin chilled with apprehension. His sour breath puffed in my face. "I will leave when I am good and ready."

"You'll leave now." A deep and deceptively mild voice from the hallway made Brom twist away from me.

Eamon stood in the hall, a plate of toast in one hand and a cup of tea in the other.

"Who are you?" Brom sneered.

"Who am I? You do not recognize your own kinsman? It has been many years, I suppose, and I've not been out and about much since my return. I believe the last time I saw you, you were about five years old." Eamon set the plate and teacup on a narrow table in the hallway and cracked his knuckles. "You have grown. So have I. Come, let me shake your hand."

Brom descended the steps, but he did not extend his hand. He peered up at Eamon, who was nearly a head taller than him, and somewhat broader in the shoulders, too. "You are that distant cousin or something, related to my father's first wife. Your name is—Ayland? Edmund?"

"Eamon."

"That's it. Eamon. Not an honest Dutch name, is it?" Brom flicked the front of Eamon's waistcoat. "We are not blood."

"No, we are not, thank the Goddess."

Brom's face twisted, his lip curling. "Get out, you and your pagan swears, before I alert the constable, or the minister. Who said you could be present here? This is a private celebration."

"That must be why the entire population of Sleepy Hollow is on the premises," Eamon said dryly. "How foolish of me. I should go. Katrina my love, your toast and tea are here when you are ready for them."

"How dare you address her in that familiar way?" spluttered Brom. "I should knock you flat, you insufferable ass!" His fist balled up, and my stomach clenched.

"Brom Van Brunt," I said sharply. "I would like you to meet my intended, Eamon Berrigan."

Brom's jaw went slack. He stared from Eamon to me and back again, blinking his pink-rimmed eyes.

"And I find it hypocritical in the extreme that you would take issue with his manner of addressing me," I continued, "when you called me a 'whore' just moments ago."

Eamon's lips retracted in a ferocious grin. "Did he now?" One massive hand gripped Brom's collar. "Come with me, *cousin*."

He hauled Brom toward the back door.

"Eamon," I called. "He lost his mother."

"I will be merciful," Eamon said between his teeth.

Smiling, I descended the steps and took a bite of the toast. It was warm, and buttery, and perfect.

The morning of my wedding, an autumn storm blew through Sleepy Hollow, shaking the remaining leaves from the trees and sending sheets of rain down the lanes, turning them to slick mud. My mother fussed and fretted, complaining that the weather was a bad omen and that we should postpone. She also objected to our plan to ride into the hills after the wedding lunch and spend some time at Eamon's cabin.

"It is very strange," she said. "You should not be leaving your fine home for a tiny cabin. You and Eamon should live here, with us. There is plenty of room."

"We will, sometimes," I reassured her. "But for a while, we would like to be alone. Surely you can understand that."

Her pale face pinked. "I suppose so. Oh, Katrina—he is very handsome, isn't he? But are you quite sure you have made the right choice?"

"I have never been more sure about anything in my life."

"Well then. But you must bring him back to our house after a few days. A week at most. We will make things comfortable for you. No daughter of mine will live in some drafty mountain cabin when she has a fine beautiful bedroom full of lovely things!"

"We will work it out, I promise." I kissed her forehead lightly. "Come now, we must hurry. We will be late to the church."

Even the gloom and the rain could not keep the denizens of Sleepy Hollow from witnessing my gossip-worthy marriage to the mysterious doctor who had saved my life. The fact that our first meeting occurred on the night of Ichabod Crane's disappearance made the event all the more alluring. So the church was crammed full of damp people, and smelled heavily of wet wool and dripping leathers.

Eamon and I spoke the words as we were prompted. We moved through the ceremony and the luncheon with smiles and thanks to those who congratulated us. But it felt like a dream—distant, and less real than the moments we had spent together in his cabin, when I was injured and he was anxious, and we had slashed at each other with words until we cut away all the layers and reached our deepest truth. Those were the moments in which we truly became one. The ceremony was important, yes, but still more vital was the ritual, conducted two nights ago in a shed at the back of our property, when I mingled my blood with Eamon's, spoke the spell with him, and painted my own neck with dripping crimson runes. It was a primal rite, and when we clasped hands at the end, I had felt the rush of magic through my body—a blazing wash of heat, a buzzing sensation over every inch of my skin.

    After that initiation into my new role as Ceannaire, our quiet ceremony in the church seemed slightly anticlimactic. But it was necessary to my future plans, and his. I could think of no better mind to partner with me when I finally took over my father's holdings—no better man to stand by my side when I set fair wages for the servants and moved toward a new reality. There would be pain and struggles we could not foresee. But as long as we stood shoulder to shoulder, we could meet it all.

    When the last guests had straggled out into the rain after the luncheon, I went to find my mother and say goodbye before my trip into the hills with Eamon. I found my father first—he was staring out the front windows and grumbling at the rain.

"You cannot go up into the hills now," he said. "Your horses will slip and fall. You will be soaked to the bone and catch a cold."

"The rain is slackening, Papa. We will be fine." I planted a kiss on his cheek. "Where is Mother?"

"In the parlor, I think."

My mother was sitting alone in a chair, clutching a soggy handkerchief. Her red-lined eyes had gone glassy from crying, and her mouth hung open a little. She stared hopelessly at the streaks and circles of mud on the floor.

"Anika would have hated this day." Her voice shook as she spoke. "She always wanted—you and Brom—"

"I know, Mother."

"I see it now—why Brom is not good for you. He drinks too much. And he is not kind, like your Eamon is."

I drew another chair close to her and sat down. "Will you be all right?"

"Oh, yes. It's these floors—all the mud. Your grandmother would roll over in her grave if she could see the state of this house. She always kept a neat household, you know. Such a fine Dutch lady, your grandmother. In these wild colonies there is only so much I can do, to keep things proper."

I hid a smile because she called our quiet little valley "wild colonies"—but I knew her distress was not really about the floors at all.

"We will return next week," I told her. "You will lose no one else, I promise. In fact, you have gained a son."

"Yes." Her face brightened. "And some little ones will arrive soon, I'll wager. Little grandchildren to run about the halls—such a cheerful prospect!"

"Mother, it is my wedding day. Kindly refrain from planning my pregnancies for another week at least."

"Oh, hush. A woman must have something to look forward to in life."

I rose from the chair, because if I stayed any longer I would tell her that a woman should create her own goals and that they need not solely center on domestic accomplishments and offspring—but then we would begin to argue, and I did not want discord on my wedding day.

Returning to the front room, I laid my hand on Eamon's arm. "We will need to delay our departure a little while."

He nodded. "How can I help?"

"Fetch a bucket of water, and I'll get a mop."

We did not leave the house until the floors were spotless, despite my mother's protests when she realized what we were doing. For all her fuss, I knew she was grateful. By the time we grabbed our bags and mounted Elatha and Nehalennia, the wind had slowed, and the rain had abated to a drizzle. Still, when we arrived at the cabin in the hills, my woolen coat and my dress were soaked through.

The place was cold and dark inside, so I took off my coat and built a fire while Eamon put Elatha and Nehalennia in the two narrow stalls out back. By the time he returned, the flames were crackling merrily, turning the cabin into the cozy sanctuary I remembered. I inhaled deeply—pine and herbs, wood smoke and horse, earth and rain. My favorite blend of scents.

"You should take off those wet things." Eamon stood behind me, a looming bulk of heat and muscle at my back.

"I fear I cannot undo all these slippery little buttons." I twisted to face him, offering my saddest expression, complete with a pouting lower lip.

He stared at the swell of my mouth. "I find myself wanting to very gently bite that lip of yours," he said. "Is that—allowed?"

"Anything is allowed now." I pushed the tantalizing lip out further and rose on my toes to reach his mouth. He took my lip in his teeth, as gently as promised, and teased it a little before kissing me soundly. A whisper of pleasure traveled through me.

"Now will you help me out of these troublesome clothes?" I turned my back to him again.

"I can try." He started at my collar, his thick fingers struggling a little over the tiny buttons of my dress. But he persisted.

"I feel that our wedding vows were lacking in some areas," he said. "For one thing, I do not expect the impossible from you."

"What do you mean?"

"In no world would I ever expect you to obey me, especially not against your own conscience."

"Thank you."

"I will tell you when I think you are wrong, of course."

"I would expect no less," I said wryly. "And I will do the same for you."

"I will respect you." He freed another button, at my waist. "And I will devote myself to your pleasure, first and always."

Longing fluttered inside me, and a tingle of sensation raced down my spine when he kissed the back of my neck. "You know we shall be the scandal of Sleepy Hollow," I said, breathless. "Everyone will think us very strange."

He shrugged. "They already do. Do you care what they think?"

"I used to be very conscious of it. I was always trying to be liked, to be wanted. But even when they all seemed fond of me, they watched me as if I were some strange creature masquerading as one of them. As if they could sense the differences between us—and not just the fashions I wore, or the position of my family—but the real differences, deep down." I sighed as the last button popped from its hole.

Eamon parted my dress at the back and pulled it down, over my shoulders. Then he laid his hand between my shoulder blades in that comforting gesture I had come to love.

"But I never needed their acceptance or approval," I continued. "As long as one person in this world understands me, and loves me as I am—I never need to care what others think of me." Eamon kissed the soft skin behind my ear, and I smiled, triumphant, reaching up to stroke his cheek. "I can do what I want now. And what I want is you. All of you." My other hand circled behind me, finding the crotch of his pants and squeezing gently.

Eamon rumbled his approval. "Well, then, wife, I think you should divest yourself of all this finery."

"My husband speaks! I must obey." Smirking, I tugged my arms out of the gown's tight sleeves and shed every other piece of restrictive clothing I had been stuffed into all day—until I stood in the center of a mountain of crumpled fabric, wearing only a pair of scandalously lacy drawers.

Eamon swept me clear of the puddled skirts and swung me onto the bed. "I see the appeal of these now." He ran his finger under the edge of the drawers. "Their presence heightens the allure of what is hidden beneath." The naughty finger drew a line right down my center, and I squirmed, sucking in a sharp breath. "Eamon, do not tease me."

"And by that you mean 'please Eamon, tease me.' " He moved his body over mine. "I plan to make this last a very long time."

"Is that so? You were rather quick to your pleasure last time."

"Well, we have all night, and the rest of our lives. We can do this again—" he kissed my forehead— "and again—" a kiss to the hollow of my throat— "and again." A long kiss on my lips.

"Remove your clothes," I ordered. "Now."

He obeyed, while I watched, reveling in the sight of his immense shoulders, deeply cut collarbones, and sleek chest muscles. His stomach was so dramatically ridged I could have used it as a washboard, and I yearned to trace those angular hips and run my hands down those powerful legs. The sheer glorious size of him loosened every muscle and joint in my body, until I was practically puddled on the bed.

Finally Eamon came to me. He washed over me like a tide of fierce love, flooded me with his heat and his caresses, until I was liquid fire under his fingers. I burned, and craved, and whimpered, while he swept his hands over my breasts and nuzzled my neck and laid a series of hot kisses down my stomach.

Then he stopped.

I opened my eyes, furious at the interruption. His cheekbones were scarlet, his beautiful mouth parted with indecision.

"What is it?" I asked.

"I want to do something, but—I am not sure it is right—"

"Eamon." I sat up and stroked his face, and danced my fingers through his black hair. "I told you, everything is allowed. Everything is right. Tell me what you want to do."

He met my gaze then, and his eyes were dark with sinful promise. "I want to kiss you *everywhere*. I know how your mouth tastes, but I want to know how all of you tastes. If you will let me."

Oh sweet heaven. The parts of me that he wanted to taste tingled with *yes*, and when I kissed him I whispered *yes* into his mouth.

Whatever reprobate instinct gave him the idea, I exalted it, praised it over and over in my mind while he indulged his impulse. Now and then he looked up at me for confirmation, which I could hardly give because I felt the euphoria approaching. My hips twisted, my legs writhed, my insides ached for something more, for a fullness.

I seized Eamon's head and pulled his face up to mine.

"Now," I hissed savagely. "I need all of you."

"I don't want to hurt you—"

"I want everything—I don't care if it hurts."

"Katrina the Irresistible." He grinned, but his voice was shaky with his own urgent desire. "How can I say no?"

I gripped his hips and guided him, my teeth clenched and my gaze fixed on his face. There was a beautiful violence in the way we collided together, merging in the way we were meant to—and the burst of pain seemed only fitting, because it was our way, he and I—pain and sorrow mixed with our pleasure and joy.

"I love you, Katrina." The Horseman's eyes blazed into mine, and I thought I saw the echo of real flames in them. I smiled, and I called him *fiend*, and *lover,* and other vicious and tender names, while we crashed together, galloping toward the brink of rapture, off the ledge into the wild delirium of night.

Printed in France by Amazon
Brétigny-sur-Orge, FR